Caddie Woodlawn

Book, Music, and Lyrics by
Susan C. Hunter
and **Tom Shelton**

Based on the book by
Carol Ryrie Brink

A SAMUEL FRENCH ACTING EDITION

SAMUEL FRENCH

FOUNDED 1830

NEW YORK HOLLYWOOD LONDON TORONTO

SAMUELFRENCH.COM

ISBN 978-0-573-69857-6   Printed in U.S.A.   #29660

RENTAL MATERIALS

An orchestration consisting of **Accordion, Violins, Cello, Bass, Clarinet, Flute, Trumpet, Harp, Banjo/Guitar**, and **Percussion** will be loaned two months prior to the production ONLY on the receipt of the Licensing Fee quoted for all performances, the rental fee and a refundable deposit.

Please contact Samuel French for perusal of the music materials as well as a performance license application.

IMPORTANT BILLING AND CREDIT REQUIREMENTS

CADDIE WOODLAWN was first produced by The Missouri Arts Council at the Landers Theatre on March 26, 1992. The performance was directed by Mick Denniston, with choreography by Chyrel Love Miller, with the musical direction of Christopher Levy, with sets and lights by John R. Rogers, and costumes by Ruthmary Denniston. The Production Stage Manager was Chuck Rogers. The cast was as follows:

ROBERT IRETON	John Johnson
MR. WOODLAWN	Roland Stevenson
MRS. WOODLAWN	Paula Patterson
REVEREND TANNER	John Flesch
YOUNG CADDIE	Julie Skiles
YOUNG TOM	Matthew Taylor
CADDIE WOODLAWN	Danna Weddell
TOM WOODLAWN	Scott Miller
CLARA WOODLAWN	Jennifer Manna
HETTY WOODLAWN	Christen Nehmer
ANNABELLE	Chelsea Sheppard
MRS. HYMAN	Jane Coughenor
KATIE HYMAN	Jackie Ross
MISS PARKER	Mandy Toler
JOHN, Dakota chief	Jeff Riley
MELVIN KENT	Mark Gideon

SETTLERS . . . . Charlie Bahn, Sandye Bates, Erin Sheppard, Sarah Thomas, Lindsey Woods, Cory Mayberry, Janelle Cobb, Kerry Taylor, Sam Matthews, Ashley Mack, Amber Creek, Debbie Stevenson, Connie Henry, Susan Peters

JOHN'S FRIENDS . . . . . Heath Harvin, Sandy Johnson, Nicci Cobb, Casey Baltes

CADDIE WOODLAWN was also produced by The Red Cedar Youth Stage on September 17, 2009. The performance was directed by Blaine Halverson with the assistance of Nikki Hoeppner, with the musical direction of Amy Wescott, and with the technical direction of Jonathan Rudenborg. The cast was as follows:

CADDIE WOODLAWN	Katie Baker
ROBERT IRETON	Aaron Knaack
JOHN WOODLAWN	John Whitman
HARRIET WOODLAWN	Theresa Boettcher
TOM WOODLAWN	Karsten Halverson
WARREN WOODLAWN	Tate Russell

CADDIE WOODLAWN, in a substantially different form, was workshopped by the Whittier (CA) Junior Theatre in August 1986 with the following cast:

CADDIE	Dawn Ramey
TOM	Justin Barber/Andy Campion
WARREN	Richie Oliver
HETTY	Annie Pickett
CLARA	Cindie Jackson
MINNIE	Emily Eiden
ANNABELLE	Melissa Harned
KATIE HYMAN	Vella Karman
YOUNG TOM	Chris Simmons
YOUNG CADDIE	Megan O'Connor
OBEDIAH JONES	Kenny Campion
MAGGIE BUNN	Sarah Karman
ASHER JONES	Jason Harris
SILAS BUNN	John Combs
LIDA SILBERNAGLE	Kathy Grobe
JANE FLUSHER	Erin Estrada
LITTLE MARY	Shannon Simmons
YOUNG WARREN	Alex Hunter
DAKOTA CHILD	Aimee Lee
EMMA McCANTRY	Christie Campion
LIZZY CUSTIS	Julia Peasley
MRS. WOODLAWN	Irene Brandenburg
MR. WOODLAWN	Michael Eiden
REVEREND TANNER	Ray Merrill
MELVIN KENT	Scott Hunter
NATE CUSTIS	Deacon Hunter
ROBERT IRETON	Tim Miller
MISS PARKER	Claire Lunbeck
UNCLE EDMUND	Tom Shelton
MRS. HYMAN	Roxie Lee
JOHN, Dakota Chief	Brad Whitfield

CHARACTERS

CADDIE WOODLAWN – A young girl, 13 years old

ROBERT IRETON – A cheery Irishman, taken to singing, dancing, and handing out good advice

JOHN WOODLAWN – Caddie's father, handsome and gentle, with quiet strength

HARRIET WOODLAWN – Caddie's mother, refined, wants the same for her children

TOM WOODLAWN – Caddie's mischievous older brother, full of fun and pranks, about 14 years old

WARREN WOODLAWN – Caddie's younger brother, about 10, always trying to keep up with the other two, full of energy

CLARA WOODLAWN – Caddie's older sister, takes after her mother, very lady-like and sweet

HETTY WOODLAWN – About 7, a tattletale and tag-along

MINNIE WOODLAWN – 5 years old, sweet-faced and happy (can double as **LITTLE HETTY** and littlest child)

ANNABELLE GRAY – Cousin to the Woodlawns, a graduate of finishing school, finds Wisconsin "quaint and rustic"

MRS. HYMAN – A snoopy neighbor

REVEREND TANNER – The Circuit Rider, hails from Boston (can double as **CHARLIE ADAMS** and **MR. WOODLAWN'S GRANDFATHER** [dancer])

KATIE HYMAN – About Caddie's age, quiet and very shy

JOHN – Caddie's friend, a Native American

MELVIN KENT – An ignorant bigot

MISS PARKER – The local schoolteacher (can double as **MR. WOODLAWN'S MOTHER** [dancer])

OBEDIAH JONES – A large, hulking bully about 14 years old, can double as **JOHN'S** friend

LITTLE TOM – Tom at age 9 (can double as **SILAS BUNN**)

LITTLE CADDIE – Caddie at age 8 (can double as **LIDA SILBERNAGLE** or **JANE FLUSHER**)

LITTLE WARREN – Warren at age 5 (can double as **SMALL CHILD SOLOIST**)

LITTLE HETTY – Hetty as a small child (Can double as **MINNIE**)

MARY WOODLAWN – A sickly child (can double as **JANE FLUSHER** or be a baby doll)

NATE CUSTIS – A friend of Melvin Kent

EZRA MCCANTRY – A friend of Nate Custis (can double as **SETTLER 1**)

MAGGIE BUNN – Caddie's best friend (can double as **MILDRED ADAMS** or **GIRL**)

LIDA SILBERNAGLE – A know-it-all

ASHUR JONES – Obediah's oafish brother (can double as **BOY**, and **MR. WOODLAWN AS A BOY**)

SILAS BUNN – Maggie's little brother, a clown

MRS. MCCANTRY – A settler (can double as **MRS. ADAMS** and **SETTLER 2**)

JANE FLUSHER – One of Caddie's friends

CHARLIE ADAMS – A new settler

MILDRED ADAMS – Charlie's daughter (can double **DAKOTA CHILD**)

MRS. ADAMS – A new settler

VARIOUS CHILDREN, SETTLERS, NATIVE AMERICANS including:

GIRL

BOY

LITTLEST CHILD

SETTLER #1

SETTLER #2

JOHN'S FRIEND

DAKOTA CHILD

MR. WOODLAWN AS A CHILD (DANCER)

MR. WOODLAWN'S MOTHER (DANCER)

MR. WOODLAWN'S GRANDFATHER (DANCER)

SCENE BREAKDOWN

NOTE: Elsewhere scenes can take place in front of curtain or on Porch set, if desired.

PROLOGUE

(A hill, overlooking a grassy riverbank in Wisconsin.)

(Lights rise on a **SOLITARY FIGURE (ROBERT IRETON)**, *silhouetted against the sky. He is plucking an idle little tune on the banjo. Taking pleasure in the melancholy mood, he begins to sing.)*

ROBERT IRETON. *(singing)*
MARK HOW THE HILLSIDE IS SILENT AND WAITING
FOR SOMETHING ABOUT TO BEGIN.
THE WORLD SEEMS TO PAUSE
AS SOMEWHERE DOWN THE VALLEY
A CHANGE IS COMING
A CHANGE IN THE WIND.

(He speaks.)

The old tales say this hillside was sacred to the woodland creatures 'fore the humans claimed it for themselves. They honored it, so says the story, for it was here the king o' the wolves gathered his kin on the bright moonlit nights to go a-huntin' in the dark forest below. But when first these eyes beheld this place, the land had changed. Settlers, callin' themselves "Americans" had raised roofs upon it and parceled it out with lines of hewn wood fences. Much of the forest had given way to ripplin' wheat, and anything in the way had been pushed further up the river. These new-comers didn't stop to contemplate the right or wrong of it. It seemed their destiny to come in and change things. But this new life changed them as well. Some grew greedy. Some grew strong. Some broke and some flourished. But all of 'em passed, leavin' at last, those things which are forever. Like this hillside, fer instance. O' course, the first day I set foot upon this soil, I wasn't contemplatin' eternity. I was thinkin' o' today, and how these Irish hands could be puttin' a morsel o' food inta this mouth 'fore the day was out. Little did I dream I'd be a-puttin' down roots. Workin' the land, pullin' life from the soil, and finally some day, sleepin' beneath it like a babe in its mother's arms. But then, that was afore I'd met up with a young lass name o' Caddie Woodlawn and her family. She was a mere slip of a thing when they arrived in Dunnville, musta been spring o' 1857. There was a wee bit of a town there then, but Mr. Woodlawn was come to build a sawmill, somethin' new to Wisconsin in those days. At that time, the Woodlawn family numbered eight. Mister and Missus, o' course, and six children. One of 'em, dear little Mary, had taken ill on the journey. So seriously that her parents held faint hope that she would ever recover. Caddie and her two brothers, Tom and Warren, took to things right off, as young'uns will, but their mother remembered the old ways in Boston. The move had not been so joyous for her. Mr. Woodlawn, though, was lookin' to the future, dreamin' o' the towns to be built, the progress to be made. It was a time o' change for Wisconsin. Every day a new family o' settlers, a new farm. Faith, you could feel change ridin' in on the wind.

(He sings.)

LOOK'A DOWN THE ROAD.
WHAT'S A'COMIN' DOWN THE ROAD
FROM YONDER?

GIRL.

IT'S A HORSE!

BOY.

IT'S A HORSE AND A WAGON!
WITH A FAMILY

GIRL.

FAMILY

BOY.

A FAMILY INSIDE!

(Other **SETTLERS** *enter, pointing toward the river.)*

SETTLER #1.

AND THE LITTLE STEAMER,

AND THE STEAMER'S CHUGGIN' IN,

SETTLER #2.

CHUGGIN' IN

A-BRINGIN' IN

ALL.

MORE PEOPLE!

GONNA TAME WISCONSIN,

GIVE IT AMERICAN PRIDE!

WELCOME, STRANGER! CAN I LEND YOU A HAND?

THERE'S LAND HERE A-PLENTY,

AND THE LIVING IS FREE.

WORKIN' WITH YOUR NEIGHBOR

HELPS TO BUILD A BRAND NEW COUNTRY.

COME ON, FRIENDS, LET'S RAISE UP THE ROOF

FOR ANOTHER NEW FAMILY!

LITTLEST CHILD. *(to* **ROBERT***)* Hey, mister. Who are you?

ROBERT. Robert Ireton's me name.

GIRL. Are you new here?

ROBERT. Just arrived this very day. I'm lookin' fer a job. Any suggestions?

BOY. There's a new family in town. The Woodlawns. We're raising the roof on their barn today. Why don't you try there?

ROBERT. That I will, me kind sir. And thanks fer the advice.

BOY. You're welcome, mister!

(All but **ROBERT** *exit.)*

ROBERT *(to audience)* And so, with such a simple beginnin', the life o' Robert Ireton was changed forever.

(snaps his fingers)

Quick as that!

(He exits as curtains open revealing the exterior of the house. **NEIGHBORS** *are busily working with hammers, saws, and paint brushes.)*

MRS. HYMAN.

> OH, MY PAPA WAS FROM LONDON
> AND MY MAMA LIVED IN PARIS

REVEREND TANNER.

> AS FOR ME, I HAILED FROM BOSTON
> TILL I LEFT IT LAST YEAR.

MISS PARKER.

> AND THE FOLKS WHO RUN THE DRY GOODS
> ALWAYS TALK ABOUT ST. LOUIE.

ALL.

> SEEMS LIKE EVERYONE'S FROM SOMEWHERE
> EVERYONE'S FROM SOMEWHERE
> EVERYONE'S FROM SOMEWHERE

MELVIN KENT.

> BUT THERE'S NO ONE FROM HERE!

> *(Dance)*

ALL.

> WELCOME, STRANGER, CAN I LEND YOU A HAND?
> THERE'S LAND HERE A-PLENTY,
> AND A PERSON IS FREE.
> DON'T MATTER WHERE YOU COME FROM,
> TIME HAS COME FOR A NEW BEGINNING.
> COME ON, FRIENDS, LET'S RAISE UP THE ROOF
> FOR ANOTHER NEW FAMILY!

NATE CUSTIS.

> CAME OUT HERE TO MAKE MY FORTUNE.

EZRA MCCANTRY.

> TRAP SOME FURS OR FARM THE LAND.

MR. WOODLAWN.

> BUILD A SAWMILL.

TANNER.

> PREACH TO ALL THE PEOPLE.

ALL.

> EVERYBODY'S GOT A DREAM.

WOMEN.

> YES, EVERYBODY'S GOT A DREAM.

MEN.

EVERYBODY'S GOT, GOT A DREAM
GREAT AND GLORIOUS,
SO COME ON,

MEN & WOMEN.

COME ON!

MEN, WOMEN & CHILDREN.

COME ON,

ALL.

FRIENDS, LET'S LEND THEM A HAND!

(Dance)

ALL.

YES SIR, NEIGHBOR, LET US LEND YOU A HAND
THERE'S LAND AND THERE'S PLENTY,
JUST AS FAR AS YOUR EYE CAN SEE.
EVERYBODY WORKING,
GONNA BUILD A BRAND NEW COUNTRY.
COME ON FRIENDS, LET'S RAISE UP THE ROOF!

MEN.

COME ON, FRIENDS, EVERYBODY RAISE THE ROOF!

WOMEN.

WELCOME, FRIENDS, LET'S RAISE UP THE ROOF
FOR ANOTHER NEW

MEN.

ANOTHER NEW

CHILDREN.

ANOTHER NEW

ALL.

ANOTHER NEW, ANOTHER NEW FAMILY!
LET'S RAISE THE ROOF!

LITTLE TOM. *(entering with paintbrush and pail)* Caddie! Caddie! Look! I get to paint the barn!

LITTLE CADDIE. Let me help!

MRS. WOODLAWN. Caroline Woodlawn, do not touch that brush!

LITTLE CADDIE. But, Mother, Tom gets to paint. Why can't I?

MRS. WOODLAWN. *(laughing)* Because you are a little girl. Painting is for men and boys.

LITTLE CADDIE. Then I wish I was never born a girl!

TANNER. For shame, child. You don't mean it, surely.

LITTLE CADDIE. Yes, I do. Boys get to do all the best things.

MRS. WOODLAWN. *(embarrassed)* Caddie! You mustn't speak so! This is Reverend Tanner, the circuit rider.

TANNER. *(Bible in hand)* I spread the good news of the Bible in the wilderness.

MRS. WOODLAWN. He used to live in Boston, just as we did. Now, apologize to him, then go to the porch to sit with Mary.

LITTLE CADDIE. Yes, Mother. I apologize, Mr. Tanner.

TANNER. *(kindly)* No harm done, my child.

LITTLE WARREN. *(rushing in with a paint brush)* Look, Caddie! I getta paint the barn!

LITTLE CADDIE. Warren, too! Mother!

MRS. WOODLAWN. Caroline Augusta Woodlawn, you heard me well enough the first time. Now, go!

LITTLE CADDIE. Yes, Mother.

TANNER. Bless my soul.

MRS. WOODLAWN. I know a child would never act like that in Boston, Reverend. But it's so...so savage here. However have you managed?

TANNER. Wisconsin will grow on you, Mrs. Woodlawn. One day, you'll wake up and wonder how you could have lived anywhere else.

MRS. WOODLAWN. Oh, Reverend, that could never happen.

TANNER. I must admit, I sometimes miss some of the comforts...

MRS. WOODLAWN. Mr. Tanner, when was the last time you had a real Boston meal with baked beans and brown bread?

TANNER. I can't remember.

MRS. WOODLAWN. Well, you shall stay the week with us, and you shall have it. Every night, if you like.

TANNER. Mrs. Woodlawn, I can taste it already.

*(**ROBERT** enters like the Pied Piper, with the **CHILDREN** at his heels. He approaches **MELVIN KENT**, and some of the other **MEN**.)*

ROBERT. Beggin' yer pardon, sirs. They call me Ireton. Robert Ireton. I was told there's a Mr. John Woodlawn who might be searchin' fer hired hands.

MR. WOODLAWN. I'm John Woodlawn. What can you do, Mr. Ireton?

ROBERT. I can milk the cows and plow the fields equal to any man alive, and I can sing and play the banjo a fair sight better 'n most.

LITTLE CADDIE. What fun! Oh, Father, hire him! Please do!

LITTLE WARREN. Yes! Yes!

MR. WOODLAWN. A singing farmhand, eh? It does sound intriguing.

MELVIN KENT. Ah, Woodlawn, you know them Irishmen never does a day's work. Too busy drinkin' and carryin' on. Worse 'n an Indian. You'll have nuthin' but trouble.

MR. WOODLAWN. Really, Mr. Kent? What do you say to that, Ireton?

ROBERT. *(with defiant dignity)* I say give me a chance to prove meself and ye'll not regret it, sir!

MR. WOODLAWN. What do you think, children? Shall we try him out?

CHILDREN. Yes! Yes!

MR. WOODLAWN. Very well, Mr. Ireton. We'll see what you're made of.

ROBERT. Thank ye, sir!

*(He skips about, playing his pennywhistle, followed by the **CHILDREN**.)*

MISS PARKER *(to **CLARA** and **LITTLE CADDIE** as they return to the porch)* Hello there, girls. I'm Miss Parker. I'll be your teacher here in Dunnville.

CLARA. My name is Clara Woodlawn, and this is my sister.

(*CLARA nudges* **CADDIE** *to answer.*)

LITTLE CADDIE. (*with an awkward curtsey*) Pleased to meet you, ma'am.

MISS PARKER. My, what a sweet little lady you are.

LITTLE CADDIE. (*indignantly*) I'm not a lady. I'm a Dakota chief!

(*All the* **BOYS** *cheer appreciatively, while* **MISS PARKER** *looks dismayed. Suddenly a group of real* **DAKOTA** *appears, hushing the crowd. They move through the wary* **SETTLERS** *until they stand before* **CADDIE** *and* **TOM**. *One of them,* **JOHN**, *curiously touches* **TOM**'s *red hair.*)

MRS. WOODLAWN. Oh, Johnny! Do something!

(**JOHN** *turns his attention to* **CADDIE**. *He smiles at her and she returns the smile. Suddenly,* **JOHN** *lifts her high into the air, staring at her flaming red locks.* **CLARA** *gasps.* **MRS. WOODLAWN** *clings fearfully to* **WARREN** *and* **MARY**.)

MRS. WOODLAWN. Oh my! Johnny!

MELVIN KENT. Hey you, Indian! Just what do you think you're doin'?

(**JOHN** *turns to his* **COMPANIONS** *and smiles. They move in curiously, touching the hair of the* **TWO CHILDREN**.)

Did you hear me, Indian? Get your hands off those children!

(**KENT** *moves aggressively toward* **JOHN** *who turns menacingly at the sound of his voice. Swiftly,* **MR. WOODLAWN** *steps between them. He smiles calmly at* **JOHN**.)

MR. WOODLAWN. (*offering his hand in friendship*) Welcome, friend.

(**JOHN** *hesitates.* **MR. WOODLAWN** *grasps his hand firmly and shakes it, smiling.* **JOHN** *smiles back.*)

JOHN. Hau koda.*

MR. WOODLAWN. Welcome.

JOHN. *(with warm welcome in his voice, touching his heart)* Cante waste nape ciyuzapo.*

MR. WOODLAWN. Harriet, bring out some food for our guests.

MRS. WOODLAWN. But Johnny...

MR. WOODLAWN. Please, Harriet. Do as I say.

MRS. WOODLAWN. Yes, Johnny. Clara.

(They move toward the house.)

MR. WOODLAWN. And smile, Harriet.

MRS. WOODLAWN. *(smiling weakly)* Yes, Johnny.

*(She and **CLARA** exit, smiles frozen on their faces. **MR. WOODLAWN** gestures towards **JOHN**'s gun.)*

MR. WOODLAWN. May I?

*(**JOHN** hands him the rifle. **MR. WOODLAWN** examines it.)*

Tom, bring me the spring lock on the porch.

*(**TOM** obeys. **MR. WOODLAWN** hands it to **JOHN**.)*

Try this. It's much more accurate than your flintlock.

*(**JOHN** examines the rifle closely, with obvious approval.)*

KENT. Are you crazy, Woodlawn?

*(**JOHN** is pleased and holds out his hand to shake with **MR. WOODLAWN**.)*

MR. WOODLAWN. It's yours, my friend.

JOHN. Pilamayaye.* Thank you.

KENT. Lord help us!

*(**MRS. WOODLAWN** and **CLARA** arrive with several pies and loaves of bread. They offer them to **JOHN'S COMPANIONS**, who immediately eat them, nodding with satisfaction.)*

LITTLE CADDIE. *(approaching **JOHN** and pointing to herself)* I'm Caddie. Caddie.

---

* For translation, please see Appendix 1 on page 116.

JOHN. *(nodding solemnly and pointing to himself)* John.

LITTLE CADDIE. Hello, John.

> *(They shake hands.* **JOHN** *gestures to a* **DAKOTA CHILD** *who brings forth a handmade doll.* **JOHN** *gives it to* **CADDIE,** *who shakes hands with the* **CHILD.***)*

Why, thank you, John. Pilamayayess.

JOHN. *(correcting her gently)* Pilamayaye. For you, Little Red Hair.

> *(One of* **JOHN'S FRIENDS** *moves to* **MR. WOODLAWN,** *shakes his hand and gives his flintlock to him. This is repeated by others.* **MR. WOODLAWN** *chuckles.)*

MR. WOODLAWN. Oh, dear. I suppose they all want spring locks now.

KENT. You're not going to do it, are you?

MR. WOODLAWN. I don't know why not. I can easily change them over.

> *(to* **JOHN***)*

I'll be happy to change these rifles for you. Come back tomorrow and I'll have them.

> *(***JOHN** *nods. He gestures to others to leave. He gestures farewell and exits, followed by his* **COMPANIONS.***)*

MRS. WOODLAWN. Oh Johnny, I was so afraid they were after a red scalp.

MR. WOODLAWN. They were only curious, my dear. I suppose they had never seen hair that color before. And really, Harriet, we were equally as curious about them, I daresay. They probably wondered why you were staring so.

LITTLE CADDIE. John wouldn't hurt us, Mother. He gave me a doll.

LITTLE TOM. He came to make friends.

MRS. WOODLAWN. We certainly are a long way from Boston. I never imagined I'd be serving my best apple pies to a group of...oh dear!

CLARA. Must we stay, Mother?

MR. WOODLAWN. Our home is here now, Clara. For better or worse.

CLARA. Not for me. Boston shall always be my home.

LITTLE TOM. Boston? Not me! This is where I want to be. There's lakes and rivers!

LITTLE WARREN. And prairies! And forests!

LITTLE CADDIE. And adventures! It's just about the most perfect place in the world!

*(Music swells into **WISCONSIN WELCOME REPRISE**)*

EVERYONE.

WELCOME, NEIGHBOR, LET US LEND YOU A HAND
THERE'S LAND HERE A-PLENTY
AND A MAN CAN BREATHE FREE.
SIDE BY SIDE TOGETHER
HELPS TO BUILD A BRAND NEW COUNTRY.
COME ON, FRIENDS, LET'S RAISE UP THE ROOF…

(The final timbers are placed on the roof. A small pine tree is placed at the top of the barn, marking the completion.)

LITTLE TOM. It's up! The roof is up!

*(**EVERYONE** cheers.)*

TANNER. My friends, let us give thanks for the bounty with which we are blessed.

(He sings.)

GOD PROTECT WISCONSIN'S CHILDREN
SAFE IN FREEDOM'S GOLDEN HAND.
MAY THEIR LIVES FOREVER FLOURISH
NURTURED BY THIS BLESSED LAND.

MR. WOODLAWN.

FROM THE LAND WE FORGE A HOME
OUR CHILDREN FEED, THE HEARTH FIRE TEND.
IN DEATH THE DUSTY EARTH ENFOLDS US
TRUE AND FAITHFUL TO THE END.

EVERYONE.

> OH, WISCONSIN, MAKE YOUR CHILDREN
> STRONG TO MEET TOMORROW'S FEARS.
> KEEP US MINDFUL OF THE BLESSINGS
> WROUGHT BY YOU THROUGH ALL THE YEARS.

> *(As the song ends, there is a sudden commotion at the porch.)*

CLARA. Mother! Come quickly! It's Mary!

MRS. WOODLAWN. *(rushing to* **MARY***)* Oh Johnny! She's burning with fever again! Take her inside! Clara, fetch some water. Quickly!

LITTLE CADDIE. *(as* **NEIGHBORS** *help carry* **MARY** *inside)* Wait for me! Let me help!

> *(She rushes toward the house, but is stopped by* **ROBERT***.)*

ROBERT. Now, now, lass. There's little you can do for her.

> *(She buries her head in his chest, sobbing.)*

LITTLE CADDIE. No! No! Mary! Oh, Mary!

> *(blackout)*

ACT ONE

Scene One

(A few weeks later on a hillside near the Woodlawn house.)

*(The strains of **GRAVESIDE HYMN** are heard. **ROBERT** enters sadly and a light appears on a new grave.)*

ROBERT. We cannot cling to what is no more. We mustn't wish for what cannot be. Oh, Mary, we must bid ye farewell too soon. Our tears mark yer passin', but 'tis nothin' can stop it.

*(Slowly, the **WOODLAWN FAMILY – FATHER, MOTHER, CLARA, LITTLE TOM, LITTLE CADDIE, LITTLE WARREN,** and **BABY HETTY** – enter, followed by **NEIGHBORS** and **MR. TANNER.**)*

TANNER.

FOR EVERYTHING THERE IS A SEASON
AND A TIME FOR EVERY MATTER UNDER HEAVEN.
A TIME TO BE BORN AND A TIME TO DIE,
A TIME TO PLANT AND A TIME TO REAP,
A TIME TO KILL AND A TIME TO HEAL,
A TIME TO LAUGH AND A TIME TO WEEP.

*(**TANNER** and **MOURNERS** sing simultaneously.)*

FOR EVERYTHING THERE IS A SEASON
AND A TIME FOR EVERY MATTER IN HEAVEN.
AHHHH.
A TIME TO SEEK, A TIME TO LOSE.
AHHHH.
A TIME THERE IS TO LOVE.

MOURNERS.

> OH, WEEP AND MOURN
> FOR A SUDDEN FROST HAS SWEPT THE LAND
> WITH AN ICY GRIP
> SOLEMN DEATH EXTENDS HIS HAND
> TO GATHER HIS HARVEST IN.
> AND THOSE WHO BEG AND THOSE WHO PRAY
> AND THOSE WHO SEEK TO RUN AWAY
> WILL FIND NO HAVEN FROM THE DAY
> WHEN DEATH HAS BECKONED THEM.

TANNER.

> A TIME TO REND AND TO SEW WHAT'S TORN,
> A TIME TO DANCE AND A TIME TO MOURN.

> *(spoken)*

> A season there is, and only God can rule the passing of one to the other.

> (**MRS. WOODLAWN** *approaches the grave, laying a flower on it and singing.*)

MRS. WOODLAWN.

> AND SUMMERS GLOW AND COME AND GO,
> AND WINTERS BLOW AND COME AND GO,
> YET NEVER MORE DO WE SEE THE ONES
> WHO DEATH HAS GATHERED IN.

MOURNERS. *(with* **MRS. WOODLAWN***)*

> AND SUMMERS GLOW AND COME AND GO
> AND WINTERS BLOW AND COME AND GO
> AND NIGHT GIVES WAY TO THE DAWNING DAY
> THAT LIFE MAY RISE AGAIN.

> (**MOURNERS** *exit quietly, leaving the* **WOODLAWN FAMILY** *and* **ROBERT** *huddled around the grave.*)

MRS. WOODLAWN. *(gaunt with grief)* Wrap your shawl more tightly, Caddie. Your fever hasn't gone.

LITTLE CADDIE. Yes, Mother.

MRS. WOODLAWN *(to* **MR. WOODLAWN***)* She looks so pale and thin. Oh, Johnny, I couldn't live if…

MR. WOODLAWN. Harriet, I've been thinking. These last weeks I kept wishing I could take Mary outside and let her breathe the fresh air; run in the sunshine.

MRS. WOODLAWN. She wasn't strong enough.

MR. WOODLAWN. No. But Caddie could be.

MRS. WOODLAWN. Caddie?

MR. WOODLAWN. Look at how frail she's grown. I want you to let me try an experiment. Let Caddie run about like the boys do.

MRS. WOODLAWN. Johnny, no!

MR. WOODLAWN. Wouldn't you rather she learned to plow than make samplers, if she can get her health by doing so?

MRS. WOODLAWN. But it isn't right or proper.

MR. WOODLAWN. We have a new life now, Harriet. Right and proper are Bostonian notions.

MRS. WOODLAWN. And good ones! A girl must learn civilized ways!

MR. WOODLAWN. Bring up the other girls as you like, but let Caddie be different.

MRS. WOODLAWN. I don't know…

MR. WOODLAWN. Harriet, until she gets her health.

(He embraces her.)

MRS. WOODLAWN. Very well. But there must come a time, Johnny, for her to learn to make samplers, too.

MR. WOODLAWN. To be sure, Harriet. To be sure. Come now. It's time to say good-bye.

*(**MRS. WOODLAWN** kneels at the grave, touching its white cross.)*

MRS. WOODLAWN. I'm ready. Clara, bring the children.

*(**ALL** exit except **LITTLE CADDIE** who kneels beside the grave, a flower in her hand. **ROBERT** looks on silently.)*

LITTLE CADDIE. Don't forget me, Mary, when you're in heaven. I'll remember you forever. I promise…forever.

(She places flower on the grave.)

ROBERT. *(as lights fade on* **LITTLE CADDIE***)* There were those who, in the livin' o' their lives, slowly forgot the tiny grave on the hill. But year on year, in spring and summer, ye could always find a fresh-picked blossom restin' upon that grassy slope, placed there by one who would always remember.

(He sings.)

AND SUMMERS GLOW AND COME AND GO
AND WINTERS BLOW AND COME AND GO,
AND SISTER'S TEARS REACH ACROSS THE YEARS
THAT LOVE MAY LINGER STILL.

Caddie! Caddie Woodlawn! Come into the house now! Yer mother wants ye!

(Lights come up on **CADDIE WOODLAWN***, now 13 years old.)*

CADDIE. Just a minute, Robert! Just one minute!

(She places a flower on the grave, just as she has done for so many years. She rises, about to leave, but is interrupted by the entrance of **TOM***, 14, and* **WARREN***, 10, who come whooping in.)*

TOM. Caddie! Hey, Caddie!

CADDIE. Over here!

WARREN. We been lookin' everywhere for ya. The Dakota have set up camp 'cross the river. See the smoke?

TOM. They're probably working on a canoe. We're gonna watch. Come on.

HETTY. Tom! Warren! Wait for me!

WARREN. *(making a face)* It's Hetty.

CADDIE. Oh, bother. She'll want to tag along.

TOM. Let's run!

(They head for the river as **HETTY***, 7, enters.)*

HETTY. There you are.

CADDIE. Too late.

HETTY. Where are you going?

WARREN. No place.

HETTY. You are, too. Tell me.

TOM. None of your business.

HETTY. Let me come, too, Tom. Please!

TOM. No.

HETTY. Why not?

TOM. Because it isn't a place for big-mouthed scaredy cats.

WARREN. Yeah! Big-mouthed scaredy cats!

HETTY. Mother says you shouldn't use such language. Just wait till she hears what you said!

CADDIE. Tattle-tale! Come on, Tom. We just have time to visit the Dakota camp before dinner.

HETTY. But it's across the river.

WARREN. So?

HETTY. You can't swim! None of you!

TOM. That's all you know! I can just touch bottom. Caddie and Warren will hang on to me.

HETTY. But what if you stumble?

TOM. *(joyfully)* We'll all be drowned! Wouldn't it be bully?

HETTY. *(exiting at a run)* I'm telling Mother.

CADDIE. Now we'll catch it.

TOM. We'll think up something. The three of us.

WARREN. Yeah, if we just stick together.

CADDIE. Mother will be angry.

TOM. We'll explain it to Father. He'll understand.

CADDIE. Yeah. And if we're punished, we'll take it like men.

WARREN. Yeah, like the Three Musketeers!

TOM. Together!

WARREN. The three of us!

CADDIE. Inseparable forever!

ALL THREE. *(sing)*
    WE ARE WE!

CADDIE.

I'M THE SAUCER,

TOM.

I'M THE CUP,

WARREN.

I'M THE TEA!

CADDIE.

AND WE'RE CLOSER THAN THE PEAS IN THE POD OF THE
SWEET GREEN PEA

ALL.

OH! WE'RE WHAT IS KNOWN AS A TRIO.

CADDIE.

YOU,

TOM.

AND YOU,

WARREN.

AND ME!

ALL.

OH!

MAKE A BEAUTIFUL MELODY.

CADDIE.

HO HO HO HO HO!

TOM.

HA HA HA HA HA

WARREN.

HEE HEE HEE HEE HEE HEE!

ALL.

WE ARE WE!

CADDIE.

I'M THE ANKLE,

TOM.

I'M THE SHIN,

WARREN.

I'M THE KNEE!

CADDIE.

WE GO DEEPER THAN THE BRAVEST OF FISH
IN THE DEEP BLUE SEA.

ALL.

OH! WE'RE WHAT IS KNOWN AS A TRIO.

TOM.

YOU!

CADDIE.

AND YOU!

WARREN.

AND ME!

ALL.

OH!

MAKE A BEAUTIFUL HARMONY!

CADDIE.

ROMEO AND JULIET

COULDA HAD A FAR BETTER FATE, I BET,

TOM.

IF, 'STEAD OF TRYING TO GO IT ALONE,

THEY HAD A CHUM TO SORT OF

WARREN.

CHAPERONE!

ALL.

WE ARE WE!

CADDIE.

I'M THE MASTER!

TOM.

I'M THE DOG!

WARREN.

I'M THE FLEA!

ALL.

WE'LL LAST LONGER THAN THE MOST FAMOUS THREE

OUT OF HISTORY,

OH!

WE MAY BE ONLY A TRIO,

CADDIE.

BUT YOU!

TOM.

AND YOU!

WARREN.

AND ME!

ALL.

OH! WE SOUND LIKE A SYMPHONY!

TOM. *(spoken)* Come on! Let's cross the river!

CADDIE. I'll race you to the water!

WARREN. Hey! Wait for me!

(They exit.)

(blackout)

Scene Two

(In One. [Porch])

(An a capella 'WE ARE WE' is heard in the distance, lacking one voice. **ROBERT** *enters, carrying a load of wood.)*

ROBERT. Tom! Warren! Caddie! Hurry in ta dinner now.

*(***TOM*** and **WARREN** *race in boisterously.)*

Whisht, lads!

WARREN. *(shouting)* Hello, Robert!

ROBERT. Whisht, I say! Where have ya been so long? It's nearly suppertime. And where's yer sister, may I ask?

TOM. Gathering hazelnuts. We found a thicket full of 'em.

WARREN. *(taking a few hazelnuts from his pocket)* We filled our pockets. See?

TOM. Caddie wanted to get more than us, so she hitched up her skirt and put 'em there.

ROBERT. Heavens o' thunder! Did ye have ta pick tonight ta pull such pranks?

TOM. What's wrong?

ROBERT. Mr. Tanner himself is a-settin' in your mother's parlor, waitin' for his supper.

TOM. The circuit rider?

ROBERT. Yes, and your mother's been askin' after Caddie all afternoon, and makin' everyone hop to, so to impress the Reverend, him bein' from Boston and all. She and Clara have run theirselves ragged fixin' up somethin' special, and herself always with an eye to the door, lookin' fer some help from Caddie.

WARREN. Is she mad?

ROBERT. She's got that grim sort o' frown she gets when she's tryin' to hold back the angry words that are dancin' on her tongue.

TOM. I'll have to think up a good one to get Caddie out of this scrape.

WARREN. Don't worry, Tom. Whatever you say, I'll nod.

TOM. Good. Robert, watch for Caddie, and warn her, will you?

ROBERT. I'll try. Hurry now. You'll just have time ta get into yer own two seats afore yer mother starts servin'. Oh, I quiver to think o' the row we'll see when yer sister comes back.

(**TOM** *and* **WARREN** *run off.* **ROBERT** *peers off anxiously.*)

(*Crossfade to Scene 3*)

Scene Three

(The interior of the Woodlawn house.)

(The large table at center is being set for supper by MINNIE, *6, and* HETTY.*)*

HETTY. Oh, Minnie, where can they be?

MINNIE. I don't know. I'm just horrendified to think what's gonna happen.

HETTY. Me, too.

MRS. WOODLAWN. Is the table set, girls?

MINNIE. Yes, Mother.

MRS. WOODLAWN. Excellent. Then we shall proceed to serve.

HETTY. But, Mother. Tom and Warren and Caddie aren't here.

MRS. WOODLAWN. *(darkly)* You know the family rules, Hetty. Meals are held for no one. Anyone missing supper will have nothing.

CLARA. But, Mother. Mr. Tanner is here.

MRS. WOODLAWN. Tonight will be the same as always, Clara. Ring the dinner bell.

(A knock is heard at the door. MINNIE *answers it.)*

MINNIE. Hello, Mrs. Hyman.

MRS. HYMAN. *(letting herself in, accompanied by her daughter,* KATIE*)* Good evening, Harriet.

MRS. WOODLAWN. Why, Rebecca Hyman. What brings you here at this hour?

MRS. HYMAN. I was just passing by as the Little Steamer docked, and I thought it'd be neighborly to ask for your mail and bring it over to you. You always have such intriguing correspondences, Harriet.

MRS. WOODLAWN. Yes. Thank you, Mrs. Hyman.

(She reaches for the letters. MRS. HYMAN *avoids her reach.)*

MRS. HYMAN. Always a letter from Boston or somewhere interesting. Got one from a Miss Annabelle Gray this time.

MRS. WOODLAWN. Do I? Well, I shall certainly have to read it later. When I have the time.

(She takes the letter.)

MRS. HYMAN. Oh, my! You're mighty busy right now, I guess. Katie and I seem to have arrived at suppertime. Reckon you have something special cooked up tonight for Reverend Tanner.

MRS. WOODLAWN. *(reluctantly)* There's plenty to go around…

MRS. HYMAN. We'd be delighted!

MRS. WOODLAWN. *(with a strained smile)* Minnie, set two more places at the table.

MINNIE. Yes, Mother.

KATIE. Let me help.

MRS. HYMAN. *(proudly)* Isn't my Katie a joy, though. Just like your girls.

(She pats **MINNIE** *on the head.)*

MRS. WOODLAWN. Why, thank you.

MRS. HYMAN. Except that Caddie, of course. She's a wild one, isn't she?

MRS. WOODLAWN. I don't know what you mean.

MRS. HYMAN. Oh, she's the terror of Dunnville. Always whooping around like some sort of crazy Indian. Katie tells me she actually punched young Obediah Jones in school yesterday.

MRS. WOODLAWN. What?

MRS. HYMAN. Gave him a bloody nose.

*(***MR. WOODLAWN*** and ***MR. TANNER*** enter.)*

MRS. WOODLAWN. I don't believe it. Hetty, is this true?

HETTY. Well, yes.

MRS. WOODLAWN. Why didn't I hear about it?

HETTY. Tom said he'd push me in a mud puddle if I told.

MRS. WOODLAWN. He did!

HETTY. Obediah deserved it, Mother. He was talking back to Miss Parker terribly.

MRS. WOODLAWN. Johnny, Caddie gave Obediah Jones a bloody nose.

MR. WOODLAWN. *(laughing)* Did she?

MRS. WOODLAWN. Johnny!

MR. WOODLAWN. I'll speak to her about it.

TANNER. Dear me!

MRS. HYMAN. Why, Reverend, I didn't notice you come in. Welcome back to Dunnville.

TANNER. Thank you, Mrs. Hyman.

MRS. HYMAN. We were just talking about Caddie.

MRS. WOODLAWN. I'm sure Mr. Tanner would much rather have his supper than stand around listening to idle gossip.

MRS. HYMAN. I notice there's a few empty places. I guess Caddie and your boys are still cross river at the Dakota camp.

MRS. WOODLAWN. What would they be doing there?

MRS. HYMAN. Heaven only knows, eh, Reverend? All I know is I saw them stripping off all their clothes and wading across at the ford.

HETTY. Yes, Mother, it's true, and Warren called me a big-mouthed...

MRS. WOODLAWN. That will do, Hetty.

MRS. HYMAN. Naked as the day they were born.

HETTY. No, Mother. They left their drawers on, truly.

MRS. HYMAN. Well, nearly naked!

MRS. WOODLAWN. *(changing the subject)* Shall we all sit down to supper?

TANNER. If my nose does not deceive me, there are Boston beans and brown bread in the offing.

MINNIE. *(as she leads* **TANNER** *to his seat)* Your nose isn't lying, Mr. Tanner.

MR. WOODLAWN. Mrs. Hyman, Katie, here are your seats.

(calling off)

Robert, more water, please! Mr. Tanner, will you ask the blessing?

(Everyone sits at the table with three spots remaining conspicuously vacant.)

TANNER. Almighty God, we beseech thee to bless this bounteous food, and to bless, also, this home. We thank thee that here in the wilderness we can find cleanliness, good manners, and all the precious graces of civilization. Grant that nothing ever disturb this peace and serenity. Amen. Upon my soul, those chairs were empty a moment ago! What have we here?

(He has opened his eyes to see **TOM** *and* **WARREN**, *who have taken their places during the prayer.* **TOM** *sits next to* **KATIE**.*)*

MR. WOODLAWN. Two more hungry mouths, Mr. Tanner. Your prayer must have raised them out of the floorboards.

MRS. HYMAN. Out of the river is more likely.

*(***ROBERT*** *enters with water.)*

TOM. Well, maybe we rushed a little.

WARREN. We didn't want to be late.

TOM. Well, any later. Gosh, Ma…I mean, Mother, if we'd known there was company…

MR. WOODLAWN. Never mind that, Tom. Where is Caddie?

TOM. Yes, sir. Let me explain about that.

MR. WOODLAWN. Please do.

TOM. Well, as I was saying, we were rushing so as not to be late. And we wouldn't have been even the tiniest bit late…if it hadn't been…for the accident!

WARREN. Accident?

TOM. *(elbowing him in the ribs)* Yes, Warren, the accident.

(sotto voce)

Just nod, remember?

WARREN. *(nodding frantically)* Yes, yes! The accident!

MRS. WOODLAWN. *(fearfully)* Tom, has something happened to Caddie?

TOM. Yes!

MRS. WOODLAWN. *(rising from the table)* Where is she? What happened?

TOM. Oh, Ma, Caddie's fine.

WARREN. *(nodding frantically)* Fine!

TOM. You see…

> *(sings)*

> WE WERE COMIN' HOME ONLY US THREE,

WARREN.

> UH HUH!

TOM.

> JUST AS LICKETY SPLIT AS A FLEA.

WARREN.

> UH HUH!

TOM.

> 'CAUSE WE KNOW HOW YOU SCOLD
> WHEN THE SUPPER GETS COLD,
> AND YOU CANNOT GUESS WHERE WE COULD BE.

WARREN.

> UH HUH!

TOM.

> BY THE RIVER WE HEARD THIS CRY,

WARREN.

> YOO HOO!

TOM.

> LIKE A YOUNG GIRL ABOUT TO DIE!

WARREN. *(correcting his cry to a more appropriate screech)*

> ACH ACH!

TOM.

> SO FAR OFF AND DISTANT, YET WILDLY INSISTENT,
> WE CERTAINLY HAD TO REPLY!

WARREN.

> GAAAH!

TOM.

> DON'T YOU SEE?
> WE WERE DUTY-BOUND TO HUNT AROUND
> AND FOLLOW THAT SOUND
> TILL THE TROUBLE WAS FOUND.
> YOU'LL AGREE
> THERE WAS NOTHING TO DO
> BUT TO FOLLOW EACH CLUE
> TILL THE GIRL WAS IN VIEW

WARREN.

> AND THE VICTIM WAS, TOO!

HETTY. *(spoken)* Who was it?

TOM. A little Dakota girl.

MINNIE. Oh my!

TOM. *(sings)*

> IN THE RIVER!
> SHE WAS GOING DOWN,
> JUST ABOUT TO DROWN,
> TILL WITH LUCK WE FOUND
> HELP TO GIVE HER!
> ON THE BANK WAS
> THIS ANCIENT CANOE,

WARREN. *(helping* **TOM** *to act it out)*

> AH HA!

TOM.

> SO WE JUMPED IN AND OFF WE FLEW!

WARREN.

> YAHOO!

TOM.

> IT WAS BEAT-UP AND CREAKY
> AND DANGEROUSLY LEAKY,
> BUT TELL US, WHAT ELSE COULD WE DO?

WARREN.

> HELP! HELP!

TOM.

> AS THE RIVER DID RAGE AND ROAR

WARREN.

> AAUGH

TOM.

WE DRAGGED HER ON BACK TO SHORE!

WARREN. *(portraying the victim)*

UGHGH!

TOM.

BUT SHE'D STOPPED ALL HER THRASHIN',

HER FACE HAD TURNED ASHEN,

WE SENSED THAT WE HAD TO DO MORE!

WARREN. *(gagging and clutching his throat)*

GAAAGH!

TOM.

CADDIE KNEW

IF WE DIDN'T ACT QUICK

THAT GIRL'D BE MORE THAN SICK,

THOUGH THE TENSION WAS THICK

SHE DEVISED UP A TRICK!

SO TRUE BLUE!

CADDIE RIPPED AT HER VEST

THEN SHE THUMPED ON HER CHEST

TOM.

WE BOYS THOUGHT IT WAS BEST

THAT WE HEAD ALONG WEST.

SO WE'RE GRIEVED CADDIE'S LATE,

BUT YOU SEE WHAT A STATE

OF CONFUSION WE FOUND

ON THE ROAD HOMEWARD BOUND,

COMING LICKETY SPLIT AS A FLEA,

CADDIE AND WARREN AND ME!

(spoken)

She'll be here shortly.

*(**KATIE** giggles. There is silence around the table.)*

MRS. WOODLAWN. *(Finally, in humiliation)* Tom Woodlawn, that's the tallest tale I've ever heard.

TOM. No, Ma...I mean, Mother. It's true, isn't it, Warren? Every word.

*(**WARREN** nods fiercely, but freezes uncertainly under **MRS. WOODLAWN**'s gaze.)*

MRS. HYMAN. Humph!

ROBERT. *(hoping to head off* **CADDIE***)* Well, I'd best be getting' outside...to me chores.

(As he exits, **CADDIE** *enters, narrowly missing a collision.)*

CADDIE. Tom! Warren! Just wait till you see how many hazelnuts I got!

(She is a bedraggled mess, clutching her skirt which is filled with hazelnuts.)

MRS. WOODLAWN. *(horrified)* Caddie!

CADDIE. Mother! Oh! Company! Mrs. Hyman! Mr. Tanner!

(In alarm, she drops the hem of her skirt and all the hazelnuts roll to the floor.)

MRS. HYMAN. My, my!

CADDIE. *(as she sees the look of humiliation on her mother's face)* I'm sorry, Mother.

MRS. WOODLAWN. *(embarrassed to the point of flight)* Excuse me, please.

(She exits.)

MR. WOODLAWN. Caddie, go and wash up.

CADDIE. Father, I never intended...

MR. WOODLAWN. The road to hell is paved with good intentions, Caddie.

CADDIE. Yes, Father.

(She exits in disgrace. The other **GIRLS** *scurry to clean up the hazelnuts and take them into the kitchen.)*

MRS. HYMAN. Wild as a heathen Indian.

MR. WOODLAWN. I do hope you're enjoying the meal my wife worked so hard to prepare, Mrs. Hyman.

MRS. HYMAN. Oh, I certainly am, Mr. Woodlawn. Most certainly.

MR. WOODLAWN. That was quite a story, Tom.

TOM. *(sheepishly)* Yes, sir.

MR. WOODLAWN. Is it entirely true?

TOM. Um, no, sir. Maybe not entirely.

MR. WOODLAWN. I don't think it's the least bit true. And you should be ashamed, both of you, for spinning bold-faced fables at the table.

MRS. HYMAN. Oh, boys will be boys, Mr. Woodlawn.

MR. WOODLAWN. *(continuing as if she hadn't spoken)* Or anywhere.

TOM & WARREN. Yes, sir.

MR. WOODLAWN. You may leave the table.

(**BOYS** *exit.*)

I apologize, friends.

TANNER. No need, no need.

MR. WOODLAWN. Have you heard news of the war on your travels, Mr. Tanner?

TANNER. *(eagerly moving on to a new subject)* Yes, yes. The armies of the Confederacy grow weaker every day, they say.

MR. WOODLAWN. Let us hope for peace in the coming year.

TANNER. Indeed.

*(Lights out as **MRS. HYMAN** wolfs down her supper, the **TWO MEN** converse, and **KATIE** stares at all the empty seats.)*

(blackout)

Scene Four

(The porch outside the Woodlawn house.)

*(**CADDIE** sits on the steps. **ROBERT** sits on a barrel playing a harmonica. **CADDIE** sighs.)*

ROBERT. Ye have the weight o' the world on yer young shoulders tonight, Miss Woodlawn.

CADDIE. I'm always doing the wrong thing.

ROBERT. Ye've had yer share o' disgraces, I'll grant ye that.

CADDIE. I guess I'll be a disgrace to Mother all my life.

ROBERT. Don't you fret too much about it, me girl. Ye'll learn the right way o' things.

CADDIE. When I grow up?

ROBERT. Somewhere around then.

CADDIE. Mother says that when she was my age, she could make bread and jelly and six kinds of cakes, not to mention all the samplers she had sewn. Clara was the same.

ROBERT. Ah, but can they plow a field?

CADDIE. I suppose not.

ROBERT. Give yerself time, Caddie. Ye'll be long enough grown when the time comes. Fer now, rejoice in what ye are.

CADDIE. If it were up to me, I'd never grow up.

ROBERT. Faith, lass. Dinna say such things. O' course, ye can always keep a bit o' the child tucked away in here.

(He touches his heart.)

But to never grow up? Why, 'twould be like the winter never makin' way fer the spring.

CADDIE. Still, I wish there was a way.

ROBERT. Whisht, child!

*(**TOM** and **WARREN** enter.)*

WARREN. There you are, Caddie.

TOM. Want an apple? We pinched some from the barrel when Pa sent us out.

CADDIE. I'm not really hungry.

WARREN. Then give it here, Tom. I'm starving.

CADDIE. What are they doing now?

TOM. Pa and Mr. Tanner are discussing news. There's more massacre talk up north.

WARREN. Mr. Tanner says everyone's gettin' nervous.

CADDIE. What did Father say?

WARREN. He thinks John and the other Dakota are our friends. He trusts them.

CADDIE. Hooray for Father!

TOM. Not Mrs. Hyman, though. She practically fainted just mentioning massacre.

CADDIE. Oh, her.

TOM. Shhh! Here they come.

TANNER. *(as* **ADULTS** *enter)* Your views are stimulating, John, if a little naïve. But now, I must escort these two lovely ladies to their rig.

MRS. HYMAN. Thank you, Reverend.

KATIE. Good-bye, Tom. I liked your story, even if it wasn't true.

TOM. Thanks.

　　　*(*ADULTS *and* KATIE *drift off.)*

CADDIE. *(imitating* **KATIE***)* Oh Tom, I simply adored your story!

WARREN. Even if it wasn't true.

　　　(He bats his eyes and makes kissing sounds.)

TOM. Button your lip, Warren.

CADDIE. She likes you, Tom.

TOM. So?

WARREN. Don't you think she's pretty?

TOM. Nah, she's a girl.

CADDIE. So am I.

TOM. Yeah, but that's different. You're not her kind of girl.

CADDIE. Well, I'm glad of that.

TOM. Me, too.

MR. WOODLAWN. *(as he and* **MRS. WOODLAWN** *re-enter)* Look at the stars Harriet, peeking through the branches.

MRS. WOODLAWN. It's beautiful, isn't it?

(She puts her hands in the pocket of her apron, and pulls out the letter delivered by **MRS. HYMAN** *earlier.)*

Oh my goodness, I nearly forgot this letter from Annabelle.

WARREN. Who?

MRS. WOODLAWN. Your cousin Annabelle Gray from Boston. I invited her to visit in my last letter to Aunt Margaret. Listen to this, everyone. "I shall be charmed to visit you, dear Aunty Harriet. Mama and Papa think that my education will not be complete without a view of the majestic open spaces of my native land. Although I have recently been finished at the Miss Blodgett's Seminary for Young Ladies, I myself feel that I may yet be able to acquire some useful information in the vicissitudes of travel." Well, well.

WARREN. Reckon Caddie couldn't write a letter like that.

CADDIE. Wouldn't want to. Sounds so prissy and silly.

MRS. WOODLAWN. Well, I for one am looking forward to seeing Cousin Annabelle.

MR. WOODLAWN. We will *all* welcome her eagerly.

MRS. WOODLAWN. And put forth our very best demeanor.

TOM. Ohh noo.

MR. WOODLAWN. *(with a look of warning to all three)* Oh, yes!

MRS. WOODLAWN. Just think, Johnny. Company from Boston! Clara will be delighted. Well, I must go in and put the little ones to bed.

MR. WOODLAWN. Mrs. Hyman is still talking poor Mr. Tanner to distraction. I'd better try to rescue him.

MRS. WOODLAWN. Watch out for flying insults.

MR. WOODLAWN. I certainly shall.

MRS. WOODLAWN *(to* **CADDIE,** *as each* **ADULT** *exits separately)* I'm sure, Caroline, that you will momentarily feel the urge to come inside and assist Clara with the supper dishes.

CADDIE. Yes, Mother.

TOM. When Cousin Annabelle comes we'll probably have to wear our Sunday suits every day.

WARREN. We'll have to act grown up. And polite.

*(***WARREN*** heaves a big sigh.)*

TOM. Sounds like Cousin Annabelle's already grown up two or three times.

CADDIE. Yecchhh.

WARREN. Are you gonna talk fancy like that when you grow up, Caddie?

CADDIE. I'm never going to grow up.

TOM. *(laughing)* You'll have to.

CADDIE. Oh? Just watch me. You can become solemn and responsible and proper like Cousin Annabelle if you want to, Tom Woodlawn, but I shall simply refuse.

TOM. Well, if you can do it, so can I!

WARREN. Me, too!

ROBERT. Hush with yer silly wishes on a moonlit night. The Devil himself will hear ye and grant them!

CADDIE. I bet we could do it if we really tried. I know! Let's make a pact!

WARREN. A what?

CADDIE. A pact! A dreadful oath! We each of us will promise the others never to grow up, no matter what.

TOM. I'll do it.

WARREN. So will I!

ROBERT. *(rising from the barrel and exiting)* Turn a deaf ear, Mr. Beelzebub. They don't mean it, truly.

CADDIE. All right, now. We must all join hands.

(They do so.)

Now, repeat after me.

(sings)

SWEAR YOU'LL NEVER GROW UP,
NEVER TURN GRAY AND OLD.
NEVER GO TO BED EARLY
WITHOUT BEING TOLD.

WARREN.

SWEAR YOU'LL ALWAYS BE JOLLY,
NEVER BOTHER OR SCOLD.

TOM.

NEVER ENDLESSLY TALK
OF LIVESTOCK YOU'VE SOLD.

CADDIE.

SWEAR
NEVER TO SHAVE,

TOM.

NEVER TO SLAVE AT YOUR CHORES.

WARREN.

SWEAR TO
ALWAYS TELL JOKES!

CADDIE.

IGNORE THE FOLKS
WHO ARE BORES.
SWEAR IT SOLEMNLY!

ALL.

NEVER GROW UP,
NEVER BREAK UP WE THREE.

TOM.

STICK TO THE END,

WARREN.

SIBLINGS AND FRIENDS,

CADDIE.

CHILDREN.
YOU!

TOM.

HIM!

WARREN.

AND ME!

CADDIE. Now, you can never, never break your promise, from this day forward.

TOM. Never.

WARREN. Never, never, ever.

(**CLARA** *enters briefly.*)

CLARA. Tom, Caddie, Warren. Mother says to come in now.

TOM. *(upon* **CLARA**'s *exit, whispering)* Never.

CADDIE. *(also whispering)* Never.

WARREN. *(shouting exuberantly)* Never!

(*The others shush him as they exit.*)

(*blackout*)

Scene Five

(Exterior of the Woodlawn house, early spring.)

(The **WOODLAWN FAMILY** *is gathered expectantly, awaiting the arrival of* **ANNABELLE**.*)*

CLARA. What is taking so long? The Little Steamer must be docked by now.

MRS. WOODLAWN. Patience, Clara.

CLARA. Oh, Mother, I'm so excited.

MRS. WOODLAWN. Yes, dear. So am I.

HETTY. Minnie! Let's pick some flowers for Annabelle. That would be proper, don't you think?

MINNIE. Yes!

(They exit.)

CLARA. What will she think of us, I wonder? Everything here is so unrefined.

CADDIE. Like this?

*(**CADDIE** nonchalantly turns a cartwheel, petticoats flying.)*

CLARA. Caddie! Do stop for once!

MRS. WOODLAWN. Oh, here they are!

CLARA. Straighten your skirt, Caddie, please do!

*(**ANNABELLE** enters breezily. Behind her, **ROBERT** and **MR. WOODLAWN** stagger on with many trunks and traveling cases. **ANNABELLE** is about **CADDIE**'s age, but her demeanor is that of an adult. She is dressed in a stylish traveling suit with an astounding number of buttons trimming the bodice. She speaks in an overly-cultured voice.)*

ANNABELLE. Aunty Harriet!

MRS. WOODLAWN. *(embracing her)* Welcome, Annabelle, to Wisconsin.

*(**HETTY** and **MINNIE** reappear with hastily-picked flowers grasped in their hands.)*

ANNABELLE. Dear me! Are these children all yours, Aunty Harriet?

MRS. WOODLAWN. There are only six. And every one precious.

ANNABELLE. Of course! Mama told me there were six. But they do look such a lot when one sees them all together, don't they?

HETTY. We picked you a nosegay.

MINNIE. *(with a curtsey, holding out the flowers to* **ANNABELLE***)* Welcome, Cousin Annabelle.

ANNABELLE. How very thoughtful of you, little girls. But do hold them for me, won't you? I should hate to stain my mitts. You've no idea what a dirty journey this has been, and what difficulty I have had in keeping clean.

*(**HETTY** and **MINNIE** retrieve their bouquets in disappointment.)*

CLARA. I can imagine. Oh, Annabelle, look! We've just had our spring dresses made. Mrs. Hyman and her daughter Katie took the patterns from pictures in Godey's Ladies Book.

ANNABELLE. Yes, we were wearing the very thing, oh, six months ago. Of course, in Boston today the fashion is buttons. Why this very frock is trimmed with eight and eighty tiny jet buttons.

WARREN. Golly! You need that many buttons to fasten up your dress?

ANNABELLE. *(laughing airily)* Of course not, little boy. They are for decoration. All the girls in Boston are wearing them now, but none have as many as I.

(scrutinizing **CLARA***'s dress)*

Your dress does have a certain quaint and rustic charm, my dear. *More* than suitable for a savage country such as this. It is truly courageous of you all to attempt a civilized existence here in the untamed wilderness. It seems such a futile effort, all in all. I do pity you.

CADDIE. Don't worry about us! We manage just fine!

MRS. WOODLAWN. Caddie, please. Now, Annabelle, how would you like to begin your stay in Wisconsin?

ANNABELLE. Well, I want you to show me everything. I desire to be just as uncivilized as you are. I shall learn to ride horseback, and milk the cows...and...salt the sheep, if that is what you do...and turn somersaults in the hay bin...and...what else do you do?

TOM. *(with a wicked wink to* **CADDIE***)* Oh, lots of things!

CADDIE. *(starting to scheme)* Oh, yes! Lots and lots of things!

ANNABELLE. But really I must take just a moment to settle myself first.

CLARA. Certainly, Annabelle. You'll be sharing my room. I'll show you the way.

ANNABELLE. Thank you.

MRS. WOODLAWN. Do let me help.

ANNABELLE. *(to* **TOM, WARREN,** *and* **CADDIE** *as she and the others exit)* Please do not depart. I shall return on the instant!

CADDIE. *(waving with grand exaggeration)* Bye, bye.

(noticing **HETTY** *and* **MINNIE***)*

Those are awful pretty nosegays you made, girls.

HETTY. Yes, they are aren't they?

MINNIE. Would you like mine?

CADDIE. Why, yes, I would. I think it would look very nice pinned here on my dress, don't you?

MINNIE. Yes!

CADDIE. And Hetty's would be just right in my hair. How does it look?

HETTY. Beautiful!

CADDIE. Thank you, girls.

MINNIE. You're welcome!

(She skips happily away as **HETTY** *hugs* **CADDIE** *and follows* **MINNIE** *off.)*

TOM. So that's *dear* Cousin Annabelle.

CADDIE. Isn't she elegant, though? "My dearest, dearest cousins, you must teach me to be quaint and rustic."

WARREN. We can show her how to ride horseback, all right. Put her on Pete.

CADDIE. Warren, everybody knows you can't ride Pete. He'll head for that low shed and knock you right off... Ohhhhhh. I don't know, Warren.

TOM. Ah, come on, Caddie. She's got it coming.

WARREN. Don't forget how she hurt Minnie and Hetty's feelings.

TOM. And said Clara's dress was out of style.

WARREN. And called us uncivilized!

TOM. It's just for a joke, Caddie. It'll be funny.

WARREN. Yeah!

CADDIE. All right, we'll do it! Here she comes. Smile, everyone.

WARREN. *(with a smiling grimace)* Like this?

CADDIE. That's perfect.

ANNABELLE. *(entering)* And now, dear cousins, when shall I have my first taste of frontier life?

CADDIE. Are you sure you're ready for it?

ANNABELLE. My dearest young cousin, I am ready for anything. After all...

(sings)

I AM A GRADUATE
OF THE HENRIETTA BLODGETT
SCHOOL FOR YOUNG LADIES
NEAR HARVARD, NOT YALE.

There, among other things, we were taught by Miss B.
THAT A MODERN YOUNG LADY
SHOULD SEEK TO SET EYES ON
A THRILLING NEW HORIZON,
AND IN THE SCHOOL OF LIFE
BE FEARLESS, NOT FRAIL.
THOUGH SOME WOULD SUGGEST
IT'S INSANE TO COME OUT WEST,

ANNABELLE. *(cont.)*

> AND THAT MISS BLODGETT
> SURELY SPOKEN IN PARABLE,
> I FIND BEING HERE
> THAT THE WILD FRONTIER IS DEAR,
> AND IT'S NOT THE LEAST BIT
> FEARSOME OR TERRIBLE!

> Quite the contrary!

> IT'S QUAINT, QUAINT, QUAINT AND RUSTIC,
> THE LAY OF THE LAND IS DIVINE!

KIDS.

> QUITE A PICTURE!

ANNABELLE.

> AND, OH! BUT IT'S CHARMING
> TO LEARN ABOUT FARMING,
> THE REARING OF POULTRY AND SWINE.

KIDS.

> FASCINATING!

ANNABELLE.

> THE PIGLETS A-SQUEALING,
> IT'S ALL SO APPEALING,
> IF I WERE AN ARTIST
> I'D PAINT

KIDS.

> VERY SWEETLY.

ANNABELLE.

> A QUAINT, QUAINT, QUAINT LITTLE PORTRAIT
> TO KEEP IT SOMEHOW FOR MINE
> OH, I WILL ADMIT
> THAT IT'S BACKWARD A BIT
> AND ESSENTIALLY HICKISH AT HEART,
> BUT YOU MUSTN'T FEEL BAD
> FOR THE THINGS YOU'VE NOT HAD,
> SUCH AS CULTURE AND BREEDING AND ART!

KIDS.

> WE ARE HEARTSICK!

ANNABELLE.

YOU'RE QUAINT, QUAINT, QUAINT AND RUSTIC,

THE NATURAL LIFE, OH MY WORD!

KIDS.

STRIKES US SPEECHLESS!

ANNABELLE.

AND HOW CAN YOU OVER-RATE

PEOPLE WHO CULTIVATE

CATTLE AND SHEEP BY THE HERD.

KIDS. *(holding their noses)*

SO DIS-STINK-TIVE!

ANNABELLE.

THE PLOWING AND PLANTING

NO LESS THAN ENCHANTING,

TO THEMSELVES EVERYONE SHOULD ACQUAINT

KIDS.

GLAD TO MEET YA!

ANNABELLE.

YOUR QUAINT, QUAINT, QUAINT LITTLE FAMILY

WITH HARDSHIPS SO BRAVELY ENDURED!

KIDS.

OH, IT'S GOOD TO KNOW

THAT WE'RE NOT REALLY SLOW,

THOUGH STUCK WAY OUT HERE IN THE WEST,

AND THAT WE'RE DISTANT COUSINS

TO FAR AWAY DOZENS

OF FOLKS WHO KNOW BETTER THAN BEST!

ANNABELLE.

CHARMING PEOPLE!

SO NOW LET US MOUNT THE BOLD STALLION!

KIDS.

NO DALLYIN'!

ANNABELLE.

AND SOON I'LL BE RIDING WITH EASE.

KIDS.

LIKE THE BREEZE!

ANNABELLE.

> YOUNG COUSINS SO DEAR TO ME
> BANISH ALL FEAR FOR ME,
> LET US GET ON WITH IT, PLEASE!

CADDIE.

> PETE IS YOUR STEED.

ANNABELLE.

> A BANAL NAME INDEED
> I SUPPOSE HE WILL BUCK?

TOM.

> NO, WE WON'T HAVE SUCH LUCK

ANNABELLE. *(spoken)* What?

WARREN.

> HE'LL PROBABLY JUST KICK.

CADDIE.

> THE POOR THING'S HALF BLIND.

ANNABELLE. *(spoken)* Oh!

CADDIE.

> WE PROMISE YOU'LL FIND, THOUGH

KIDS.

> THE RIDE WILL BE MOST QUAINT AND RUSTIC!

CADDIE. *(spoken)* Right this way, Cousin Annabelle.

TOM. Let me give you a leg up.

WARREN. Bon voyage.

> (**ANNABELLE** *and* **TOM** *exit.* **CADDIE** *and* **WARREN**
> *wave encouragingly.* **TOM** *runs on to watch gleefully. A*
> ***MUSICAL INTERLUDE*** *tells the story of* **ANNABELLE***'s*
> *wild ride. Behind the rows of corn in the background,*
> *we see* **ANNABELLE***'s fashionable bonnet bobbing wildly*
> *across the stage, ending with a scream.* **ANNABELLE**
> *limps on, quite bedraggled.)*

ANNABELLE. I don't quite understand what happened. I
thought I was going along so well. In Boston, I'm sure
horses never behave like that.

TOM. Would you like to try a different horse?

ANNABELLE. Oh no! Not today, at least. Could not we salt the sheep now, perhaps?

CADDIE. Why, yes, I believe we could.

WARREN. *(rushing off)* I'll get the salt.

ANNABELLE. How charming! Will they eat out of my hand?

TOM. Sure. They're crazy about salt. Just do as you like, Cousin Annabelle.

ANNABELLE. Well, of course, I should prefer to let the cunning little lambs eat it right out of my hands.

WARREN. *(entering breathlessly and handing cake of salt to* **ANNABELLE** *with a courtly bow)* Here is the salt, dear cousin.

TOM. *(imitating* **WARREN** *'s elegance)* Shall we proceed to the sheep pen?

ANNABELLE. It's so good of you to let me.

(She and **TOM** *exit as* **OTHERS** *watch. Another* **MUSICAL INTERLUDE**. *Behind a fence we see* **ANNABELLE** *approach the* **SHEEP** *(puppets). As* **ANNABELLE** *ad libs comments, the* **SHEEP** *begin to climb all over her, trying to get at the salt. She is pulled out of sight to the ground by their enthusiasm. There is a scream and* **ANNABELLE** *re-enters. The buttons are gone from her dress and her stylish hat is missing.* **TOM** *follows her on.)*

ANNABELLE. *(nearly hysterical)* Oh! My buttons! There were eight and eighty of them! Six more than Bessie Beasley had, and now the sheep have eaten them up, every one!

CADDIE. You shouldn't have held the salt up over your head.

ANNABELLE. But they were treading upon my toes and climbing over each other to get nearer to the salt.

TOM. You should have dropped it and run.

ANNABELLE. I tried, but they were crowding in about me and *(recovering her usual composure)* Oh, what a... *quaint* experience! They'll hardly believe it when I tell them about it in Boston!

KIDS. *(singing)*

SO WHAT'S YOUR OPINION OF FARMING?

ANNABELLE. *(bravely)*

IT'S CHARMING.

KIDS.

AND HOW 'BOUT THE LAY OF THE LAND?

ANNABELLE.

IT'S GRAND!

KIDS.

AND WHAT IS YOUR FEELING

FOR PIGS WHEN THEY'RE SQUEALING

OR SHEEP WHEN THEY EAT FROM YOUR HAND?

ANNABELLE.

TOO QUAINT!

KIDS.

AND HOW ABOUT WHEN YOU WENT RIDING?

ANNABELLE.

EXCITING!

KIDS.

SO HOW DO YOU LIKE DEAR OLD PETE?

ANNABELLE.

HE'S SWEET.

KIDS.

DESCRIBE YOUR EMOTION

WHEN HE GOT THE NOTION

TO KNOCK YOU RIGHT OUT OF YOUR SEAT!

ANNABELLE.

NEARLY FAINTED.

KIDS. *(simultaneously with* **ANNABELLE***)*

WE'RE QUAINT, QUAINT, QUAINT AND RUSTIC

THE FLORA AND FAUNA'S A TREAT!

THE CATTLE ARE MOOING,

THE BLACKSMITH IS SHOEING

OUR DARLING OLD HORSE, MR. PETE.

HE MAY BE A PLUG

BUT WE'LL GIVE HIM A HUG,

JUST ABANDONING ALL OUR RESTRAINT!

ANNABELLE. *(Simultaneously with* **KIDS**.*)*

NOTHING QUITE SO ABSURD
COULD HAPPEN IN BOSTON
SO FAR AWAY
FROM HERE IT'S EXHAUSTING
TO THINK OF, OH WHERE
IS MY AFTERNOON TEA?
AND MY CHOCOLATE ECLAIR?

ALL.

WE'LL SAY WE'RE
QUAINT, QUAINT, QUAINT AND CHARMING
SO QUAINT, QUAINT, IT'S ALMOST ALARMING,

*(***TOM*** puts an egg down the back of* **ANNABELLE***'s dress.)*

SO BOSTON AND CAIRO AND PARIS WE AIN'T,
WE'RE QUAINT, QUAINT, QUAINT!

KIDS.

NOW ISN'T IT SWEET?

(they slap **ANNABELLE** *on the back)*

ANNABELLE. *(with a screech)* Ewww! What is that?

WARREN. *(laughing)* It's just an egg.

ANNABELLE. Raw?

WARREN. *(laughing even harder)* Yeah! It's a joke! See?

ANNABELLE. But it's squishy! I cannot bear squishy things! Is this an example of frontier humor? Oh my! Oh my! It's all so very...

THE OTHER THREE. Quaint and...

MRS. WOODLAWN *(entering and standing aghast at the condition of* **ANNABELLE***'s dress)* Annabelle! My goodness, child, what has happened?

THE OTHER THREE. Mother!

MRS. WOODLAWN. What is going on here? Caddie? Tom?

CADDIE. Mother...we...

ANNABELLE. *(trying to make the best of things)* Oh...nothing, Aunty Harriet. I...I have simply been...exploring the wild Wisconsin way of life, as I hoped I could. And tomorrow, perhaps, your...charming children will introduce me to the indigenous people of the woodland regions?

CADDIE. Whatever you like, Annabelle.

ANNABELLE. But for now, I believe I will retire upstairs to change into something a bit more...

WARREN. Quaint and rustic?

ANNABELLE. Yes.

MRS. WOODLAWN. *(exiting with* **ANNABELLE***)* Let me help you, dear.

CADDIE. Well, she's not a cry-baby, at any rate. Maybe we shouldn't play any more tricks on her.

TOM. *(innocently)* Of course not. But you heard her. She wants to meet the undigestible people of the woodlands.

WARREN. Huh?

TOM. John and his tribe.

CADDIE. So?

TOM. So, we'll have to cross the river to get to their camp.

CADDIE. Yes?

TOM. So, I can't wait to see all her five petticoats, and her fancy dress, and those "cunning little shoes" of hers balanced on the top of her feathered hat. How about you?

WARREN. Oh yes!

CADDIE. But Mother will be watching us.

TOM. We'll sneak out at dawn, before anyone is up. Tell Annabelle it's a Wisconsin custom.

CADDIE. All right.

TOM. *(mysteriously)* We meet at dawn.

CADDIE & WARREN. Yes!

(blackout)

Scene Six

(Hillside. Dawn the next day.)

*(***TOM, WARREN,*** *and* ***CADDIE*** *enter stealthily, followed by* ***ANNABELLE,*** *dressed to kill in her version of a safari outfit.)*

WARREN. *(full voice)* Gosh, I betcha we're awake even before the chickens.

TOM. Shhhh! Quiet, Warren.

ANNABELLE. Are you certain we shall alarm no one by our early departure?

TOM. Nah, not as long as we're careful.

CADDIE. *(nudging* ***WARREN****)* And quiet. This too is a common frontier ritual, cousin Annabelle.

HETTY. *(entering sleepily)* Where are you going?

ANNABELLE. We are venturing forth into the untamed Wisconsin wilds.

HETTY. Crossing the river?

CADDIE. Not necessarily.

HETTY. I'm going, too!

TOM. No, you're not.

HETTY. I am! I am!

WARREN. Go play with your doll.

HETTY. Mother!

TOM. Shhh! All right, Hetty. You can come.

HETTY. *(aghast)* I can?

TOM. Sure. But first we got to get some provisions, you know.

HETTY. All right.

TOM. Now, you're in charge of getting a rope and a knife.

CADDIE. *(catching on to the joke)* And an apple apiece for each of us.

TOM. We'll get the rest of the stuff ourselves. Everyone ready?

HETTY. Yes!

TOM. All right. We'll separate and meet back here in five minutes. Go!

(**HETTY** *flies off.*)

Come on, everybody.

ANNABELLE. Mustn't we wait for Henrietta?

TOM. Nah, she'll catch up in a minute.

ANNABELLE. I see.

WARREN. It's just a joke.

ANNABELLE. Rather like the humorous incidents we indulged in yesterday.

TOM. That's right.

ANNABELLE. Playing pranks seems to be a charming western custom, as well.

TOM. You could say so.

ANNABELLE. Might I try it sometime, do you think?

CADDIE. Sure, go right ahead.

ANNABELLE. Oh my! I have never done anything humorous before. I shall have to think very hard.

TOM. Of course you will. Come on. Let's go.

(*They exit. After a moment,* **ROBERT** *enters sleepily, carrying a water pail.* **HETTY** *enters breathlessly.*)

HETTY. I've got the knife and rope...Robert, have you seen Caddie and Tom and Warren?

ROBERT. No. Can't say that I have.

HETTY. Not anywhere? Not in the barn? Or behind the house?

ROBERT. Not anywhere.

HETTY. (*her face clouding with anger*) They must have left without me. Oh, they'll be sorry for this. They'll be sorry!

(*blackout*)

Scene Seven

(On the riverbank, a little while later.)

*(***CADDIE*** *and* ***ANNABELLE*** *enter.* ***ANNABELLE*** *is concentrating on the flight of a passing bird.)*

ANNABELLE. *(delirious with delight)* Ectopistes Migratorius! Commonly known as the passenger pigeon.

CADDIE. That's not a passenger pigeon. It's too late in the year.

ANNABELLE. Dearest Caroline, you are speaking to the president of the Young Ladies' Birdwatching and Wildlife Observation Society. I recognized it at once from my extensive study of western air fowl.

CADDIE. The passenger pigeons fly through in autumn.

ANNABELLE. Oh, won't Bessie Beasley be livid when I tell her about this!

CADDIE. Here's the raft. We could have just waded across with Tom and Warren. They're probably at the camp by now.

ANNABELLE. Yes, charming as your custom of fording the river with your clothing atop your head may be, you'll understand my reluctance to do so in the presence of members of the masculine gender.

(She pulls a small sketch pad from her drawstring purse.)

CADDIE. What are you doing now?

ANNABELLE. Sketching the countryside.

CADDIE. I suppose you're president of the Young Ladies' Artistic Society, too?

ANNABELLE. Certainly not! Cordelia Endicott is far more qualified than I. Why, she has been to Paris!

CADDIE. Of course she has.

*(***ANNABELLE*** *hums lightly while sketching.* ***JOHN*** *appears suddenly.)*

John!

ANNABELLE. What? Oh!

CADDIE. It's John! He's Dakota.

ANNABELLE. Yes, so he is. Oh, my! He…He is so very large! And savage!

CADDIE. Not a bit. He's my friend.

ANNABELLE. Friend?

CADDIE. Of course. What else would he be?

ANNABELLE. Why, I thought people just sort of viewed them from afar. In their habitat.

CADDIE. Like watching birds?

ANNABELLE. Well, yes. No! Not precisely. But I had no idea one actually befriended them.

CADDIE. *(disgusted)* Well, one does. Hau koda, John.

JOHN. Hau koda, Little Red Hair.

CADDIE. John, this is my cousin, Annabelle Gray. From Boston.

(**JOHN** *holds out his hand to shake.*)

ANNABELLE. What does he want?

JOHN. *(as if delivering a simple language lesson)* Napeyuze.*

CADDIE. He wants to shake hands.

ANNABELLE. *(as she daintily takes his hand)* Napeyuze. Extraordinary!

CADDIE. We are crossing the river on the raft. I yuwega.*

JOHN. *(The language lesson playfully continues.)* Hiya! No, Little Red Hair. Iwakta ye.

CADDIE. *(as if trying to show off her knowledge)* Taku yaka?*

JOHN. *(still the teacher, but also trying to get his message across)* There is danger. Okokipe.*

CADDIE. Why?

JOHN. *(gesturing to show a lightning storm is coming)* A storm comes. Wakiyan towa pi. Inahni!* Hurry to your home.

CADDIE. Thank you, John. Pilamayaye.

ANNABELLE. *(attempting to join the conversation, coquettishly)* Why, Mr. John, what a lovely belt. Is it made of animal

---

* For translation, please see Appendix 1 on page 114.

pelts? Or...dear me are those actually...human... scalps? You've taken all those yourself?

JOHN. *(smiling and shaking his head)* Hiya.

CADDIE. John doesn't take scalps, Annabelle. His father gave that belt to him. Like an heirloom.

JOHN. Go now, Little Red Hair. Iyaye. Wacagnus.

CADDIE. We will, John. Pilamayaye.

(JOHN leaves.)

ANNABELLE. Remarkable.

CADDIE. We should head home.

ANNABELLE. Nonsense! We have only begun to adventure. Did you construct this raft yourself?

CADDIE. Yes. I hope John finds Tom and Warren and sends them home, too.

ANNABELLE. Caroline, I see no signs of bad weather. Do you?

CADDIE. Not yet, but if John says...

ANNABELLE. What is this vessel put together with? Pegs?

CADDIE. Yes, that's the way the Dakota do it.

ANNABELLE. Oh well, then, I suppose it would be treacherous to cross the river on such a craft.

CADDIE. *(offended)* It's perfectly safe. You can bet on that.

ANNABELLE. Gambling! Another western pastime, I believe!

CADDIE. I didn't actually mean...

ANNABELLE. *(her face brightening with feeble mischief)* Excellent! I shall wager you one silver dollar that you cannot cross the river and back without getting wet.

CADDIE. You don't have to bet money. I'll do it for the dare.

ANNABELLE. Oh, how very adventurous of you!

CADDIE. Just let me take off my shoes.

ANNABELLE. *(a plan hatching)* Yes, of course, but please remove yourself to those bushes.

CADDIE. Why?

ANNABELLE. Oh my! Because it isn't proper to undress out here in the open.

CADDIE. It's only my shoes.

ANNABELLE. I really must insist, dear cousin.

CADDIE. Oh, very well.

(**CADDIE** *exits. As soon as she disappears,* **ANNABELLE** *giggles wickedly and runs to the raft. She removes the pegs.* **CADDIE** *re-enters and* **ANNABELLE** *straightens quickly.*)

ANNABELLE. All set?

CADDIE. All set!

ANNABELLE. Splendid! Now, remember, over and back without a drop.

CADDIE. I've done it a million times!

(**CADDIE** *boards the raft and pushes off, disappearing around a bend.*)

ANNABELLE. Oh, won't the girls faint with amusement when I relate this little anecdote.

(calling)

How are you doing?

CADDIE. *(from off)* Just fine! I'm halfway there already.

ANNABELLE. Forge on, dear cousin!

CADDIE. The raft! What's happening? It's coming apart! The logs!

ANNABELLE. *(all a-giggle)* What's that? I can't hear you! Is there a problem?

CADDIE. The pegs are gone! Oh! Oh no! Help!

(a splash)

ANNABELLE. Are your feet getting damp, dear cousin?

CADDIE. Help! Help! I can't swim!

ANNABELLE. What did you say?

CADDIE. I can't swim!

ANNABELLE. Can't swim? But I naturally assumed that all pioneer children had been instructed in the fundamentals of water safety.

CADDIE. *(amid the sounds of wild splashing)* Help!

ANNABELLE. *(swiftly removing shoes, and hat without seeking refuge in the bushes)* Never fear, dear cousin. You are fortunate to be in the presence of the champion of the Young Ladies' Swimming and Water Sports Tournament – two years consecutively!

(She takes several deep breaths, then plunges into the river just as **MR. WOODLAWN, MRS. WOODLAWN, HETTY, TOM,** *and* **WARREN** *enter hurriedly. Lightning and thunder as the storm JOHN warned of approaches.)*

HETTY. Here they are, Father.

MRS. WOODLAWN. What in the world is going on?

*(***ANNABELLE** *drags* **CADDIE,** *gasping for air, onto the riverbank.)*

Caroline Augusta Woodlawn! What have you done to your poor cousin now!

End of Act One

ACT TWO

Scene One

(Interior of the Woodlawn house, several days later.)

*(**CADDIE** lies on the sofa, reading quietly. **MINNIE** and **CLARA** enter carrying baskets.)*

MINNIE. If Greta and Brownie have laid, there will be six eggs today in the nests.

CLARA. Then I shall make a cake.

MINNIE. Might I help, Clara?

CLARA. You can measure the sugar, and stir, if you like.

MINNIE. Oh yes! Hello, Robert!

ROBERT. *(entering with the mail, grabbing **MINNIE** and swinging her above his head)* Good day to ye, Mistress Woodlawn. Off to do chores, I see.

MINNIE. I'm to collect the eggs all by myself. Clara says so.

ROBERT. Well, it's a solemn responsibility. Ye must promise to be gentle, and not fluster the hens as ye do it.

MINNIE. Cross my heart.

ROBERT. Well then, good luck to ye. Miss Caddie, yer lookin' a bit hardier today, I must say.

CADDIE. I'm feeling much better.

CLARA. She's been begging Mother to let her get up.

CADDIE. I'm as good as new.

ROBERT. Probably what yer mother is afeared of.

CADDIE. It's not fair. Annabelle played a joke on me, but I'm the one who has to suffer with this pokey old cold. And Mother blames it all on me, of course.

ROBERT. Ye shouldn't a been tryin' to cross the river when ye can't swim a stroke.

CLARA. What if you'd drowned, Caddie?

ROBERT. Where would ya be then, d'ya think?

CADDIE. I thought you'd understand, Robert.

ROBERT. I do, lass. But I can see yer mother's side, too. She nearly lost another child, ye know.

CADDIE. I guess so.

ROBERT. So stay outta mischief, an' perhaps she'll let ye out tomorrow.

CADDIE. I'll be good, I promise.

ROBERT. *(with a wink at* **MINNIE***)* Well, that'll be somethin' new.

*(***MRS. WOODLAWN*** enters.)*

The mail. Little Steamer docked this mornin'.

MRS. WOODLAWN. *(hopefully)* Anything from Boston?

ROBERT. *(as he exits)* Not this trip.

MRS. WOODLAWN. *(with obvious disappointment)* Oh. Well, perhaps next time.

CLARA. *(who has been looking through the mail)* Here's a letter addressed to Father. It's from England.

MRS. WOODLAWN. *(taking the letter)* England? What can they possibly want of him?

CLARA. Who?

MRS. WOODLAWN. Never mind. It's probably nothing important. Clara. Minnie. On to your chores.

CLARA. *(as they exit)* Oh, how I wish Father were home this very minute! England! Just think of it!

MINNIE. What's England?

CLARA. An elegant sort of place.

MINNIE. More elegant than Boston?

CLARA. Yes! England has duchesses and dukes and kings and queens.

MINNIE. What can they want with Father?

MRS. WOODLAWN. Now, girls, we'll all know soon enough. Off you go.

CLARA. Oh, Minnie! England! England! England!

(She grabs **MINNIE** *and waltzes elegantly offstage with her.)*

MRS. WOODLAWN. *(touching* **CADDIE** *'s forehead)* Your fever is gone. That's a very good sign. You'll be up and about before you know it.

CADDIE. Mother... You were disappointed just now when there was no letter from Boston, weren't you?

MRS. WOODLAWN. I suppose I was, a bit.

CADDIE. Why do you miss Boston so much?

MRS. WOODLAWN. Oh, I don't miss it, really. And anyway, there's no going back, is there?

CADDIE. Then why do you wait so eagerly for news of Boston?

MRS. WOODLAWN. I do long, sometimes, for the older, gentler ways.

CADDIE. Why?

MRS. WOODLAWN. There is a strength in tradition, Caddie. It connects you to the past. It holds a family together.

CADDIE. How can it do that?

MRS. WOODLAWN. Well, for instance, the Caroline Table is part of our family tradition.

CADDIE. *(following her mother to a small table)* It's to be mine someday, isn't it?

MRS. WOODLAWN. Yes. To look at it, it is nothing but a small table made of ordinary wood. But in our family, it is a symbol of something far greater. Many, many years ago, this table was made for one of my ancestors, whose name was Caroline. And ever since that time it has been left to the Carolines of the family as an heirloom. In each generation, a daughter has been given the name of Caroline in honor of this family tradition. Your Aunt Kitty has left it to you, as you may leave it to your little Caroline, and so on generation after generation until, someday, perhaps a hundred years from now, a little girl you have never met will see this table and be told the story of her great great great grandmother Caddie who kept the tradition alive for those who would follow.

CADDIE. How lovely Mother. It's almost like living forever.

MRS. WOODLAWN. *(smiling)* Yes. Almost.

CADDIE. Tradition. That's what Boston means to you?

MRS. WOODLAWN. That and so much more.

(sings)

THERE'S A PLACE I REMEMBER LIKE A CITY OF GOLD
WHERE THE STREETS WERE PAVED WITH WONDER
THOUGH THE COBBLESTONES WERE OLD.
AND THE AIR WAS WARM WITH PROMISE,
THOUGH THE WINDS FROM THE WATER WERE COLD.

THE CITY WAS BOSTON,
AND LIFE WAS A DAILY WHIRL,
SPINNING ROUND THE HEART OF
A YOUNG YANKEE GIRL.
THE CITY WAS WONDROUS
TO MY WILLING EYES.
EVERY BRICK, EVERY STONE
WITH A MAGIC SHONE.
THIS WAS MY BOSTON,
THIS MY PRIVILEGE, MY PRIZE.

I CAN STILL SEE OUR HOUSE
LIKE IT'S YESTERDAY.
I CAN STILL FEEL THE BREEZES
OFF OF MASSACHUSETTS BAY.
I CAN STILL HEAR THE MUSIC
OF A WHALER'S SONG.
I SUSPECT IT WASN'T HEAVEN
BUT I COULD BE WRONG.

I WOULD WALK TILL THE DAWN
ON THE ESPLANADE
I WOULD DANCE WITH THE OFFICERS
AT FANCY MASQUERADES.
I WOULD TALK TO MY FATHER

OF IMPORTANT THINGS
LIKE THE WISDOM AND RICHES
THAT TRADITION BRINGS.

THE CITY'S KNOWN GREAT THINGS,
THE CITY HAS HISTORY.
A FRACTION OF A MOMENT
IN THAT HISTORY WAS ME.
AND THOUGH IT IS DISTANT,
IT IS NEVER FAR.
FOR IT'S HARD TO ERASE
THE POWER OF A PLACE
WHERE YOU FIRST LEARNED TO WISH
ON THE EVENING STAR.
AND THE OLDER I GROW
I ONLY COME TO KNOW,
A CITY LIKE BOSTON
MAKES YOU WHAT YOU ARE.

CADDIE. That's how I feel about Wisconsin. Like it's the most beautiful place in the world.

MRS. WOODLAWN. I know, dear.

CADDIE. Couldn't you ever come to love it here as much as you love it there?

MRS. WOODLAWN. No matter where I live, Boston will always be home to my heart.

CADDIE. I understand. If ever I had to go away, I'd never forget Wisconsin.

(*sings*)

FOR THOUGH IT WERE DISTANT
IT WOULD NOT BE FAR

BOTH.

FOR IT'S HARD TO ERASE
THE POWER OF A PLACE
WHERE YOU FIRST LEARNED TO WISH
ON THE EVENING STAR,

CADDIE.

AND THE OLDER I GROW
I ONLY COME TO KNOW

MRS. WOODLAWN.

> A CITY LIKE BOSTON

CADDIE.

> A PLACE LIKE WISCONSIN

BOTH.

> MAKES YOU WHAT YOU ARE.

> *(CLARA, MINNIE, and ANNABELLE enter.)*

ANNABELLE. I found these two in the barn hunting eggs, precisely as if it were Easter.

MINNIE. *(holding her finger to be kissed)* Old Rosie pecked at my finger.

MRS. WOODLAWN. *(kissing it tenderly)* Poor little finger.

MR. WOODLAWN. *(entering with HETTY, TOM, and WARREN, who slinks in like a guilty dog)* Look who I picked up on the way home from the sawmill.

HETTY. *(breathlessly)* Mother! Mother! You'll never guess what happened in school today.

> *(MR. WOODLAWN moves to read the mail.)*

WARREN. It wasn't anything, Big Mouth.

HETTY. But it was! Everyone in school was laughing at him, even the Hankinsons!

WARREN. It was just a mistake.

HETTY. And Obediah Jones even called him stupid. Imagine Obediah Jones thinking anyone was stupider than he is.

MRS. WOODLAWN. Hetty!

HETTY. Well, he is, Mother. He's bigger than anyone else in the whole entire school, yet he can't get even the simplest lessons right. If Miss Parker wasn't so afraid of him, she'd throw him out of school, surely.

CADDIE. But what happened to Warren?

WARREN. It was my day to recite.

CADDIE. Oh yes, you've been practicing your piece all week. "If at first you don't succeed, try, try again".

WARREN. Tom's been teasing me so about it, and twisting the words all around and everything.

TOM. It really was my fault. Sorry, Warren.

HETTY. When Warren got up to recite, he said it Tom's way instead. He said, "If at first you fricassee, fry, fry a hen"!

MINNIE. *(in horror)* Oh no!

HETTY. And then Miss Parker got very red and irritable. But she gave him another chance to say it right.

CLARA. And?

WARREN. I tried! Really I did!

HETTY. *(laughing with delight)* He said it wrong again!

WARREN. It got me confused.

HETTY. That was when Obediah called him stupid, and of course Tom had to defend Warren, didn't he? Even though Mother doesn't approve of him fighting.

MRS. WOODLAWN. Oh, Tom, I hope you didn't…

HETTY. Tom and Obediah were just about to have at each other, when the funniest thing happened.

CADDIE. What?

HETTY. Katie Hyman suddenly cried out, "Oh no, Tom! Don't fight! You mustn't".

CADDIE. Katie Hyman?

HETTY. Yes! And when she said that, Tom just walked away, leaving Obediah standing there with his mouth wide open.

CADDIE. Why would you do that, Tom?

TOM. *(intensely embarrassed)* It wasn't anything.

HETTY. Oh, yes it was!

TOM. I'd promised Mother.

CADDIE. *(disgusted)* If I'd been there, I wouldn't have let Obediah get away with it.

TOM. *(bristling)* Oh, you wouldn't, would you?

CADDIE. No!

ANNABELLE. Miss Blodgett maintains that no circumstance is so dire as to resort to violence against a fellow creature.

CADDIE. Well, Miss Blodgett doesn't know Obediah Jones.

MRS. WOODLAWN. Caddie! I, for one, am proud of you, Tom. It takes the maturity of a young man to walk away from a fight.

CADDIE. But Tom isn't a man, Mother. He's a boy.

MRS. WOODLAWN. He soon will be, Caddie.

CADDIE. No you won't. Will you, Tom?

TOM. *(defiantly)* Mother's right. You've got to grow up sometime.

CADDIE. Grow up? No!

MRS. WOODLAWN. As for you, Warren, I hope you'll redeem yourself next time the family honor is at stake.

WARREN. I will, Mother, I promise!

*(**MR. WOODLAWN**, who has been reading quietly, sits down, in obvious agitation.)*

CLARA. Father, what's wrong?

MINNIE. Is it the letter from England, father?

MRS. WOODLAWN. Johnny, what do they want?

MR. WOODLAWN. They want me to come back. To England.

TOM. England? Why?

MR. WOODLAWN. That's where I was born, Tom.

MRS. WOODLAWN. Johnny, perhaps you should tell them. Everything.

MR. WOODLAWN. It all happened so long ago. Another lifetime.

CADDIE. What do you mean?

MR. WOODLAWN. I never told you, children, but I come from a family of great wealth.

CLARA. You do?

MR. WOODLAWN. But I never knew a day of ease. The pride of an old man kept me from that.

*(As **MR. WOODLAWN** sings, the lights dim and a pantomimic dance enacts the story.)*

WITH A CLICK CLACKETY, CLICK CLACKETY
CLOGS ON THE COBBLESTONES FLEW.

TINY CLICK CLACKETY, CLOGS CLATTERING
COME HEAR MY SONG, FRIEND,
AND TOSS ME A COPPER OR TWO.

I WAS BORN FAR AWAY
TO A WORLD VERY DIFFERENT FROM HERE,
WHERE A MAN'S LIFE IS MEASURED
BY BIRTHRIGHT AND LAND,
NOT BY WEALTH OF HIS SOUL
OR WORK OF HIS HAND,
AND A FAMILY'S PRIDE IS HELD DEAR.

HOW PROUD WAS MY GRANDFATHER
LIVING IN COMFORT AND EASE
IN A HOUSE WITH GREAT TURRETS
AND A LAKE FILLED WITH SWANS,
AND A GARDEN WITH PEACOCKS
THAT STRUTTED THE LAWNS,
AND SERVANTS WITH ORDERS TO PLEASE.

THOUGH MY MOTHER WAS POOR,
SEWING CLOTHES FOR A TRADE,
STILL MY FATHER ADORED HER
AND A MARRIAGE WAS MADE,
IN DEFIANCE OF ALL
THAT MY GRANDFATHER SAID.
SO HE SENT THEM AWAY
AND DECLARED THEY WERE DEAD
TO HIM, ALL FOR A FAMILY'S PRIDE!
ALL FOR A FAMILY'S PRIDE!

SO THEY NEVER RETURNED
AND MY FATHER DIED WHEN I WAS FIVE.
WEARING BREECHES AND CLOGS
I WOULD DANCE IN THE SQUARE,
LIKE AN APE ON A CHAIN,
AND THE PEOPLE WOULD STARE,
AND THROW COINS,

THAT WAS HOW WE'D SURVIVE.
WITH A CLICK CLACKETY, CLICK CLACKETY
CLOGS ON THE COBBLESTONES FLEW!
TINY CLICK CLACKETY, CLOGS CLATTERING,
COME HEAR MY SONG, FRIEND,
AND TOSS ME A COPPER OR TWO.

TOM. What about your grandfather? Did anyone tell him about you?

MR. WOODLAWN. Oh, he knew.

MRS. WOODLAWN. *(indignantly)* He simply chose to ignore his obligations to his own kin!

HETTY. Your mother should have asked for his help, Father. He would have listened, surely!

MR. WOODLAWN. She did.

CADDIE. What happened?

MR. WOODLAWN. *(sings)*
ONLY ONCE DID I SEE IT,
THAT MANSION SO STATELY AND GRAND.
THROUGH THE BARS ON THE GATE
MOTHER HELD ME TO SEE
MY GRANDFATHER STANDING ALONE BY A TREE
FEEDING PEACOCKS,
WHO ATE FROM HIS HAND.

MOTHER CALLED TO HIM SOFTLY
WITH TEARS IN HER EYES.
MY GRANDFATHER STRAIGHTENED
AND STARED WITH SURPRISE.
THERE WAS SOMETHING, IT SEEMED,
THAT HE STARTED TO SAY,
BUT HE TURNED TOWARD THE HOUSE
AND HE HURRIED AWAY
LEAVING US ON THE PAVEMENT OUTSIDE.
ALL FOR A FAMILY'S PRIDE.

CADDIE. Such a horrible old man.

CLARA. What did your mother do then?

MR. WOODLAWN. She vowed that her son would grow up able to make his own way in the world, never relying on the charity of others. And so I have, children.

(sings)

THOUGH THE OLD MAN AND I
NEVER MET FACE TO FACE,
HE TAUGHT ME A LESSON
THAT TIME CAN'T ERASE.
WHEN A MAN LOOKS TO PRIDE AS HIS ONLY TRUE FRIEND,
THOUGH HE LIVES IN A MANSION,
HE'LL FIND IN THE END
HE'S AS DARK AS A GRAVEYARD INSIDE.
ALONE WITH HIS FAMILY PRIDE!

WITH A CLICK CLACKETY, CLICK CLACKETY
CLOGS ON THE COBBLESTONES FLEW.
TINY CLICK CLACKETY, CLOGS CLATTERING,
COME HEAR MY SONG, FRIEND,
AND TOSS ME A COPPER OR TWO.

CLARA. Oh, Father, might we all have been lords and ladies if you had been accepted by the old man?

MR. WOODLAWN. Yes.

ANNABELLE. How charming to live in a mansion with peacocks and swans.

MRS. WOODLAWN. *(who has been reading the letter)* It seems we may still be given that opportunity, children.

HETTY. How?

MRS. WOODLAWN. Your father's cousin has died without an heir. It says in the letter that he may now become Lord Woodlawn.

CLARA. Lord Woodlawn!

MR. WOODLAWN. Not so fast, Clara. There is one stipulation. In order for me to accept my inheritance, I must return to England and take up residence in the old family estate.

CADDIE. Leave Wisconsin?

MR. WOODLAWN. Yes.

WARREN. You mean, forever?

MR. WOODLAWN. I'm afraid so.

(There is a stunned silence.)

This is a decision which will be quite difficult to make. I believe every one of us should have a say in it.

MINNIE. Even me, Father?

MR. WOODLAWN. Yes, Minnie. It will affect your life even more than it does mine or your mother's, for you are young.

MINNIE. Should we still be Americans, Father, if we went?

MR. WOODLAWN. No, Minnie, we'd be English.

ANNABELLE. *(excited)* Of course you shall be presented to the Queen, and there will be balls and concerts, and all manner of elegant things. Oh, I do hope you will have me to visit you there. Perhaps I will meet a wealthy duke looking for a charming, well-bred bride. Fancy an English lord coming from Dunnville. Was ever anything more unusual?

HETTY. Peacocks on the lawn, Caddie!

CADDIE. Yes, and bars on the gates!

MINNIE. Couldn't we be half American, Father? Only half?

MELVIN KENT. *(from off)* I ain't gonna wait! This is an emergency! Woodlawn!

ROBERT. *(as KENT pushes his way into the room)* Mr. Kent, there's young ones...

MR. WOODLAWN. *(rising in greeting)* Mr. Kent. To what do we owe...

KENT. I got news for you, Woodlawn. News that you, in particular, should find interesting.

MR. WOODLAWN. And what might that be?

KENT. Massacree.

MR. WOODLAWN. What?

KENT. Word from up north. The Indians is comin' and they'll be takin' scalps with 'em when they go.

MR. WOODLAWN. I don't believe it.

KENT. *(with a derisive sneer)* Well now, that don't make it any less true, do it?

CADDIE. Not John's tribe! John would never attack us!

KENT. All of 'em, Missee. I reckon they been plannin' it for months. They all got secret ways of communicatin', you know. Neighbors are thinkin' to meet here since it's the biggest house around. Any objections?

MR. WOODLAWN. No, of course not.

MRS. WOODLAWN. We'll make room for everyone somehow.

KENT. All right. We gotta get organized. Folks'll be comin' over directly. Let's go, Ireton.

(The **MEN** *exit.)*

ANNABELLE. You will forgive my naiveté, but I am simply not familiar with this word "massacree."

MRS. WOODLAWN. *(with ill-disguised apprehension)* The Dakota, dear. There is a rumor they may be planning an attack.

ANNABELLE. *(wide-eyed)* Ohhh.

MRS. WOODLAWN. We must begin preparations to protect ourselves at once.

ANNABELLE. Oh?

MRS. WOODLAWN. You mustn't worry, dear. I'm sure…Well, I'm so sorry this had to happen during your visit with us.

ANNABELLE. Oh. Not at all. Indeed, it's really awfully, awfully quaint and…Oh!

(She stares ahead in a state of disbelief.)

(blackout)

Scene Two

(Outside the Woodlawn house.)

*(**SETTLERS** scurry about fearfully, preparing for the massacree.)*

SETTLERS. *(singing)*
WAITING!
WAITING AND WONDERING
WHAT IS THIS THAT'S HAPPENING

KENT.
TO ME!

MEN.
TO US!

ALL.
TONIGHT!?

MRS. HYMAN.
ISN'T IT STRANGE TO BE
WAITING?

KATIE.
WAITING FOR, PRAYING FOR
SOMETHING *NOT* TO HAPPEN

MRS. HYMAN.
TO ME

KATIE.
TO US

BOTH.
TONIGHT!

MRS. HYMAN. Hurry along, Katie. The Indians may attack at any minute.

KATIE. Yes, Mama.

*(She drops her bundle as **TOM** passes, carrying a pail of water.)*

TOM. Here, let me take that.

KATIE. Oh no, Tom. You have your own load to carry.

TOM. Aw, it's nothing. Really!

KATIE. *(with a sweet smile)* Thank you.

MRS. HYMAN. Katie!

KATIE. Yes, Mama.

(They exit as more **SETTLERS** *enter.)*

KIDS. *(singing)*
HOW DO YOU PREPARE
FOR A THING THAT MAYBE ISN'T THERE
AT ALL?.

MAGGIE.
A SCARE

LIDA.
LIKE A SHADOW ON THE WALL?

ADULTS.
HOW DO YOU PRETEND
THAT YOU'RE NOT AFRAID
WHEN IN THE END

NATE.
YOU KNOW
YOU ARE

MRS. HYMAN.
YOU'LL BE?

HETTY. *(speaking to her know-it-all friend,* **LIDA SILBERNAGLE***)* I told everyone as soon as I heard. Do you think we'll all be scalped?

LIDA. Yes, I do. A lot of us, anyway. The rest will surely be tortured!

HETTY. *(as* **CLARA** *enters with quilts and pillows)* Oh my goodness! Clara! Lida says we're going to be tortured!

CLARA. Gracious, I don't think so. That's why we're all here. To protect each other.

HETTY. Lida, Clara says you're wrong.

LIDA. Well, what does she know?

*(***MISS PARKER** *and* **MINNIE** *enter.)*

MISS PARKER. Girls, girls, we mustn't argue at a time like this! Please!

CLARA. *(sings)*

> ONLY YESTERDAY
> I WAS FRETTING 'BOUT THE RAIN.

MISS PARKER.

> I WAS SWEATING OUT THE PAIN
> OF A CRICK IN MY ARM.

MINNIE.

> BRING BACK YESTERDAY.

OTHERS.

> GIVE US YESTERDAY.

MINNIE.

> WHO WOULD GRIPE ABOUT THE WEATHER

OTHERS.

> BEING HOME AGAIN TOGETHER
> AND SAFE FROM HARM

HETTY.

> AND FINALLY FREE OF THIS...

> *(All* **SETTLERS** *enter.)*

ALL.

> WAITING!
> WAITING AND WONDERING
> WHY THIS DARK AND DIFFERENT DANGER
> NOW

OBEDIAH.

> TO ME

ALL.

> TONIGHT?
> WAITING!
> WAITING FOR THE MOMENT
> THAT I WAKE
> AND KNOW
> THIS ISN'T REALLY HAPPENING.
> IT'S ALL A DREAM
> A SHADOW ON THE WALL.

ROBERT.

> A SCARE

CLARA.

A HOAX

ALL.

IT ISN'T REALLY THERE.

MRS. HYMAN.

I SHUT MY EYES

CADDIE.

AND DREAM A DIFFERENT SORT OF DREAM

MRS. WOODLAWN.

OF PEACE,

WOMEN.

FOR US,

ALL.

TONIGHT!

MISS PARKER. *(spoken)* Obediah Jones, help these girls with their blankets, please.

OBEDIAH. *(as he stands idly by)* I'm busy.

MISS PARKER. Doing what?

OBEDIAH. That's my business, not yours.

CADDIE. Do as Miss Parker says, Obediah.

OBEDIAH. Who's gonn 'ter make me? You? Miss Parker? I ain't scared of her, not me. Come on, Ashur.

(He nudges a large slovenly **BOY** *next to him. They start to leave. As* **OBEDIAH** *passes next to* **CADDIE,** *he suddenly trips, as if someone has put a foot out in front of him.)*

What? Hey!

(He lunges angrily at **CADDIE.***)*

CADDIE. Oh, sorry.

OBEDIAH. You will be!

MISS PARKER. Children, please. Please. Never mind, Obediah. We'll manage by ourselves.

*(***OBEDIAH** *and* **ASHUR** *lurch off.)*

MAGGIE BUNN. Oh, that Obediah Jones makes me so mad! You would think on a day like this he would try to behave.

MISS PARKER. Maggie, Caddie, we really can use some help setting up bedding in the barn.

MAGGIE. Yes, Miss Parker.

*(**OTHERS** exit. **CADDIE** lingers behind to scoop up a few blankets. **TOM** enters, not noticing **CADDIE**. He moves to **KATIE**, who is nearby and shyly holds out an elaborately-carved wooden doll – his own handiwork.)*

TOM. *(self-consciously)* I made this myself.

KATIE. It's wonderful!

TOM. I made it for you.

KATIE. *(surprised and pleased)* Tom! Why, thank you.

(She takes his hand briefly, then is suddenly overwhelmed with shyness and runs off.)

TOM. *(singing, obviously in love)*
WHAT IS THIS MELODY?
HUMMING IN MY HEART?
WHISTLING ON THE WIND
AND CALLING ME, CALLING ME TO DANCE
TO A NEW SONG WITHIN ME?

AND WHO IS THIS GIRL?
QUIET, SOFT, MYSTERIOUS,
HOLDING OUT HER HAND,
LOOKING PAST THE BOY
AND CALLING TO THE MAN.

SAYING TIME TO THINK,
TIME TO CHANGE,
TIME TO START TO
LOOK BEYOND THE BOY
AND FIND THE MAN.

*(He turns dreamily to see **CADDIE** staring in horror at **TOM**'s betrayal. **TOM** moves toward her. She backs away.)*

TOM. Caddie? Ah, come on, Caddie.

*(**CADDIE** runs off. **TOM** follows her, nearly colliding with*

MELVIN KENT *as he enters with* OBEDIAH, ASHUR,
EZRA MCCANTRY, *and* NATE CUSTIS. MR. WOODLAWN
enters separately, unnoticed.)

KENT *(to* TOM*)* Whoa, there, boy. Not so hot-headed fast.

TOM. *(speeding away)* Sorry, Mr. Kent.

KENT. We're nothin' but sittin' ducks, boys. Them Indians'll
raise our scalps before this night's out 'less we take
matters into our own hands.

MR. WOODLAWN. You're spreading alarm unnecessarily, Mr.
Kent. So far, there has been no sign of trouble.

KENT. Maybe not, Woodlawn, but they're out there, waitin'
their chance.

(CADDIE *enters with a whoop, followed by* WARREN,
MAGGIE, SILAS BUNN, *and* JANE FLUSHER. *The* MEN
swing toward the sound, ready to shoot their rifles.)

WARREN. Don't shoot!

KENT. Ah, it's only that Woodlawn girl.

MR. WOODLAWN. Caddie, you could have gotten yourself
killed.

WARREN. She was just letting off steam.

SILAS. Put a clothespin on her mouth.

CADDIE. Sorry, Father.

(The CHILDREN *move away to play quietly.)*

NATE. This waitin' sets my teeth on edge.

KENT. Well I, for one ain't waitin' much longer.

ASHUR. What'cha mean?

MR. WOODLAWN. He means we'd best return to our lookout
posts before anything happens. Don't you, Mr. Kent?

KENT. Maybe I do, and maybe I don't.

MR. WOODLAWN. Now see here. This scare may be nothing
more than tavern rumor. We wouldn't want to start
trouble where none existed before.

MCCANTRY. He's right, Melvin. We don't know anything for
sure.

KENT. Well, go on then, boys. But keep a lookout.

(The **MEN** *exit in various directions,* **KENT** *tripping noisily over a stool. The others point their rifles nervously toward him. He raises his hands in surrender. They relax and exit.* **OBEDIAH** *and* **ASHUR** *are stopped by the entrance of* **MISS PARKER**.)*

MISS PARKER. Come and wash up now, children. A massacre is no excuse to neglect the virtue of cleanliness.

(to **OBEDIAH** *and* **ASHUR**)*

You, too, boys. Come wash up.

OBEDIAH. Me?

MISS PARKER. (*apprehensively*) Yes.

OBEDIAH. Hear that, Ashur? Teacher wants us to "wash up."

MISS PARKER. (*faltering*) If you please.

(OBEDIAH *laughs and spits on the ground at* **MISS PARKER***'s feet.)*

CADDIE. Stop that!

OBEDIAH. Make me!

CADDIE. I will!

(In a flash, **OBEDIAH** *and* **CADDIE** *are at each other, punching and kicking.* **OBEDIAH** *grabs* **CADDIE***'s hair. They wrestle fiercely.)*

MAGGIE. Get him, Caddie!

SILAS. Kick him in the knee!

WARREN. Yeah!

(MRS. WOODLAWN *enters as a* **CROWD** *gathers. She is appalled at the sight that meets her eyes.)*

MRS. WOODLAWN. Caroline Woodlawn! Stop this at once!

(The fight continues. **MR. WOODLAWN, ROBERT,** *and* **TOM** *have entered.)*

Stop at once, I say!

(ROBERT *pulls* **OBEDIAH** *away by the seat of his pants as* **TOM** *retrieves* **CADDIE**.)*

Caroline Augusta Woodlawn, stand forth!

MAGGIE. He started it, ma'am.

SILAS. He was sassing Miss Parker!

MRS. WOODLAWN. Whatever the reason, there is no excuse for such behavior. That a daughter of mine should so far forget herself in her hospitality to a guest – that she should neglect her duties as a lady! Shame to her! Shame! Leave us this instant!

*(*MRS. WOODLAWN *is trembling with rage.* CADDIE *looks to her father for intervention, but he does not respond.)*

CADDIE. Father?

MRS. WOODLAWN. *(also appealing for support)* Johnny!

MR. WOODLAWN. *(as the* CROWD *watches)* Do as your mother says, Caddie.

CADDIE. It's not fair! He started it! You know it's not fair!

(She exits, sobbing wildly. **MRS. WOODLAWN** *sets her jaw resolutely.)*

MRS. WOODLAWN *(to a* SETTLER*)* I believe there is room for your blankets in the barn, Emma.

EMMA MCCANTRY. Thank you kindly, Harriet.

MRS. HYMAN. *(entering with a ladle in her hand as everyone stares)* Shall we eat?

(blackout)

Scene Three

(The same, later.)

*(**CADDIE** sits brooding by herself. **TOM** enters. He moves toward **CADDIE**.)*

TOM. Gosh, Caddie, I'm sorry about what happened.

CADDIE. *(miserably)* Leave me alone.

TOM. Well, I think Ma was wrong.

CADDIE. I said leave me alone! Why don't you go talk to your girlfriend.

*(imitating **KATIE**)* "Oh, Tom! You're so big and manly!"

TOM. *(wounded)* Have it your way!

*(He exits. **CADDIE** buries her face in her hands. After a moment, **MELVIN KENT**, **NATE CUSTIS**, and **EZRA MCCANTRY** enter stealthily, unaware of **CADDIE**'s presence.)*

KENT. Where's Woodlawn?

NATE. He and some others have gone fer more supplies.

KENT. It's plagued irksome to wait. The thing to do is attack them Indians first.

MCCANTRY. Yes. Before they come for us, let's strike hard. I know where John and his tribe are camped up the river.

KENT. Let's wipe 'em out. The country would be better off without 'em. We could sleep peacefully in our beds at night.

NATE. But there's others besides John's tribe. They might come after us from the west.

KENT. It'd be a start. If we kill these 'uns, it'll be a warning to others that we deal hard with Indians here.

NATE. Teach 'em a good lesson.

KENT. Let 'em say the men of Dunnville massacree the Indians stead 'a waitin' to be massacreed first.

MCCANTRY. Woodlawn'll be against it.

KENT. If we get enough men to our way of thinkin', we don't need Woodlawn. Our scalps is at stake! Wipe 'em out is what I say. Are you with me?

MCCANTRY. I am.

NATE. Me, too.

KENT. Good. Now spread out and talk to some of the others. We'll strike at sundown.

NATE. They'll never know what hit 'em.

KENT. Go on, now.

(They exit. **CADDIE** *emerges from the shadows.)*

CADDIE. John! Good, gentle John! My friend. If only Father were here to stop them! But he's not. It's up to me.

(She grabs a bridle lying on a bench nearby. As she does, **HETTY** *and* **KATIE** *enter.)*

KATIE. Caddie, what are you doing?

CADDIE. Katie, they're going to kill John and his people because he hasn't come to kill us. I've got to warn him!

HETTY. You wouldn't go out there now!

KATIE. Caddie! You mustn't do that!

CADDIE. I've got to. They must have a chance to get away.

HETTY. No!

CADDIE. You mustn't tell a soul where I've gone, either of you.

KATIE. But Caddie…

CADDIE. Cross your hearts.

HETTY. Oh, Caddie, don't go! Don't!

CADDIE. *(grabbing* **HETTY** *by the shoulders)* Hetty Woodlawn, innocent people are going to be murdered. If you so much as open your mouth while I'm gone, I'll…I'll never forgive you or speak to you again! Ever! Now, cross your hearts! Katie Hyman?

KATIE. *(reluctantly)* Cross my heart.

CADDIE. Hetty?

HETTY. Can't I even tell Mother?

CADDIE. Especially not her! You always say you can keep a secret, Hetty. Well, now is the time to do it. Well?

HETTY. *(wide-eyed with fear)* Cross my heart. I won't tell. I promise.

CADDIE. *(with a quick hug to* **HETTY** *and a squeeze of* **KATIE***'s hand)* Good. I've got to go. Oh, if only I'm not too late!

(She exits quickly.)

HETTY. Oh, Katie, I'm so frightened.

KATIE. No matter what, Hetty, we mustn't tell. We crossed our hearts.

HETTY. *(in awe)* We crossed our hearts.

(The **GIRLS** *stare off in silence.)*

(blackout)

Scene Four

(The interior of the Woodlawn house, hours later.)

(The voice of a **SMALL CHILD** *sings* **WISCONSIN ANTHEM**. *Slowly the lights rise on a group of terrified* **WOMEN** *and* **CHILDREN** *huddled together.)*

SMALL CHILD.

GOD PROTECT WISCONSIN'S CHILDREN,
SAFE IN FREEDOM'S GOLDEN HAND.
MAY THEIR LIVES FOREVER FLOURISH,
NURTURED BY THIS BLESSED LAND.

CHILDREN.

FROM THE LAND WE FORGE A HOME,
OUR CHILDREN FEED, THE HEARTH FIRE TEND,
IN DEATH THE DUSTY EARTH ENFOLDS US,
TRUE AND FAITHFUL TO THE END.

ALL.

OH, WISCONSIN, MAKE YOUR CHILDREN
STRONG TO MEET TOMORROW'S FEARS.
KEEP US MINDFUL OF THE BLESSINGS
WROUGHT BY YOU THROUGH ALL THE YEARS.

MRS. HYMAN. What time is it?

MISS PARKER. A little after nine, I would guess.

MRS. HYMAN. And still no sign of the child. It's as plain as the nose on your face she's been kidnapped. We'll never see her alive again.

MISS PARKER. Hush, Rebecca.

MRS. HYMAN. Remember how the whole lot of 'em were always a-grabbin' at that red hair of hers? Just waiting to add it to their scalp belts. And it won't stop there, I warrant. Once they start their bloody business, they won't rest until all our scalps are hanging next to hers!

CLARA. No! No!

MRS. HYMAN. She brought it on herself, of course. If she'd been any sort of normal girl, she'd never have run off without telling anyone, taking a horse for a ride at such a time.

MRS. WOODLAWN. I sent her away. It's all my fault.

MISS PARKER. The men are searching for her. We have no reason to lose hope. Not yet.

MRS. HYMAN. Yes, the men are gone. We are left practically defenseless, all because of that thoughtless child!

HETTY. It's not true!

MRS. WOODLAWN. What?

HETTY. I mean…Caddie must have had a good reason for doing what she did.

KATIE. Yes!

MRS. WOODLAWN. Did she say anything to any of you before she left? Anything at all?

KATIE. *(in a whisper to* **HETTY***)* I can't bear it any longer. She should have been back hours ago.

HETTY. *(whispering)* We promised, Katie. We crossed our hearts.

LIDA. I think Caddie's a traitor. She's gone off to lead the Dakota back to attack us. She thinks that way she'll save herself.

MAGGIE. Caddie would never do that! I bet she's gone off to act like a distraction. She's going to be a human sacrifice so that we all may live. She's a heroine!

LIDA. I say she's a traitor!

MAGGIE. A heroine!

MISS PARKER. Girls, please!

CLARA. I can't stand it! I hate this country, this life! If Caddie's been killed, won't we be sorry? Won't we wish we'd never left Boston?

(There is a bump outside. **EVERYONE** *reacts.)*

JANE. What was that?

SILAS. It's them! Hold on to your hair!

MISS PARKER. To your weapons, ladies!

(The **CHILDREN** *scream and cry while the* **WOMEN** *try their best to protect them.* **ROBERT IRETON** *enters, carrying two pails of milk. He narrowly misses a whack from* **MRS. HYMAN***.)*

ROBERT. What's this?

WARREN. Oh, Robert, it's you!

ROBERT. Well, o' course it's me. D'ye think Old Bessie herself would be bringin' her milk for the babes, now?

MINNIE. We thought you were coming to massacree us.

ROBERT. Did ye?

WARREN. We thought we were done for.

ROBERT. I see. That reminds me of what young Matthew O'Grady was a-thinkin' when he was surrounded by wolves one dark night in Ireland. But I suppose this is not the proper time nor place fer a tale such as that.

MRS. WOODLAWN. Tell it, Robert. It will keep the children's minds off the trouble.

ROBERT. It might at that. Very well. Gather round for the tale of O'Grady's Fiddle.

(sings)

WELL, YOUNG MATTHEW O'GRADY
COULD CHARM ANY LADY,
PRIM, PROPER, OR SHADY,
IT MATTERED NOT WHO.
WHEN O'GRADY WOULD DIDDLE
AROUND ON HIS FIDDLE,
THEY'D STOP IN THE MIDDLE
OF WHAT THEY WERE DOING.

O'GRADY WAS BLESSED WITH A GIFT FROM ABOVE
MUCH STRONGER THAN AVARICE, HATRED, OR LOVE,
FOR WHEN MATTY'D TAKE HOLD OF HIS FIDDLE 'N' BOW,
THE FOLKS'D START DANCIN' WHEREVER HE'D GO!

IN THE MOMENTS OF STRIFE
BETWEEN HUSBAND AND WIFE,
THIS GIFT SAVED THE LIFE
OF O'GRADY AND MATE.
FOR WITH MUSIC'S ENHANCIN'
THEY SOON WOULD BE DANCIN'
WHICH LED TO ROMANCIN'
NOT BREAKIN' THE PLATE!

ALL.

> FOR O'GRADY WAS BLESSED WITH A GIFT FROM ABOVE
> MUCH STRONGER THAN AVARICE, HATRED, OR LOVE.

ROBERT.

> 'TIS SAID THAT THE LANDLORD EACH REVENUE DAY
> WAS PROUD TO TAKE MUSIC INSTEAD OF HIS PAY!
>
> MATTHEW WAS KING O' THE FROLIC!
> 'TIS SAID HE COULD CURE A BABE'S COLIC,
> ARCH THE FLAT OF YOUR FOOT,
> CHARM THE WART FROM YOUR NOSE,
> EVEN CHANGE THE DIRECTION
> THE WINTER WIND BLOWS.
>
> WELL THE STORY IS TOLD,
> ON A NIGHT DARK AND COLD,
> MATTY'S FIDDLE MADE BOLD
> TILL THE HOURS WERE WEE.
> GOIN' HOME BY DUNN'S FERRY
> WHERE NONE DARED TO TARRY,
> HE WANDERED, UNWARY,
> AT QUARTER TA THREE
> WHEN HE CAME UPON
> FIVE HUNGRY WOLVES IN A PACK,
> AND ANOTHER THREE BARIN'
> THEIR FANGS AT HIS BACK!
> MATTY'S KNEES TOOK TO KNOCKIN'
> BOTH HITHER AND FRO
> AS HE TIGHTENED EACH STRING
> AND HE ROSINED THE BOW!

> *(dance)*

> WITH A FIDDLEDEE FADDLEDEE
> FODDLEDEE DERRY,
> THOSE WOLVES TOOK TO DANCIN'
> ALL OVER DUNN'S FERRY,
> AND NOW THAT HIS FAME
> TO THE CREATURES IS KNOWN,
> HE PLAYS AT THEIR WEDDIN'S
> AS WELL AS OUR OWN!

ALL.

WITH A FIDDLEDEE, FADDLEDEE, FODDLEDEE DEE,

ROBERT.

MATTY'S FAME WILL GO DOWN
IN THE WORLD'S HISTORY!

*(All applaud as **ROBERT** takes a sweeping bow. His moment of glory is cut short by a scream from **KATIE**.)*

KATIE. Oh! Oh my!

*(**JOHN**'s face appears at a window. The **CHILDREN** scream, as the **WOMEN** protect them.)*

MRS. HYMAN. This is it! This is the end!

*(She faints into **ROBERT**'s arms. He tries unsuccessfully to extricate himself.)*

MRS. WOODLAWN. Wait! It's John. He has Caddie!

*(**JOHN** and **CADDIE** enter. **MRS. WOODLAWN** rushes to her as **JOHN** steps aside.)*

Caddie! Oh my dear sweet child! Are you all right?

CADDIE. Yes, Mother, I'm fine.

MAGGIE. Where have you been?

SILAS. Did they take you prisoner?

MRS. WOODLAWN. Did they hurt you in any way?

HETTY. I see lanterns. The men are coming back!

MRS. HYMAN. *(suddenly revived)* They won't let you go, Indian, so don't try anything!

MRS. WOODLAWN. There will be no violence in my house, Mrs. Hyman.

MRS. HYMAN. Ezra! Melvin! Over here! We have one of 'em hostage!

CADDIE. No! John is our friend! The Dakota mean no harm!

MRS. HYMAN. *(brushing **CADDIE** aside)* You'll pay, Indian! Just you wait!

MRS. WOODLAWN. Go, John. Hurry! While you can.

(**CADDIE** *hugs* **JOHN** *quickly. He moves to the door, but is stopped by* **MELVIN KENT** *and several other* **MEN**.)

KENT. Good Lord! We got him! It's the chief, too!

(*He raises his rifle.* **CADDIE** *rushes toward* **JOHN**, *but is stopped by* **MRS. WOODLAWN**.)

CADDIE. No! No!

MRS. WOODLAWN. Put away your gun, Mr. Kent.

KENT. Not on your life!

CADDIE. (*breaking loose and running to* **JOHN**) I won't let you touch him!

KENT. Move outta the way!

CADDIE. He came in peace to show that the Dakota are our friends.

KENT. (*raising his rifle, ready to fire*) I said move!

(**JOHN** *reacts swiftly, throwing* **CADDIE** *out of harm's way and drawing his knife.* **MR. WOODLAWN** *and other* **MEN** *enter as* **WOMEN** *scream and* **ROBERT** *grabs* **CADDIE** *holding her back.*)

NATE. Whoa there!

KENT. Let's get him, boys!

MRS. WOODLAWN. (*suddenly bold, stepping between* **JOHN** *and* **KENT**) Stop! There will be no violence against any guest in my house! We are civilized people, Mr. Kent! And you will stop this savagery at once!

KENT. This is men's business. Out of the way!

(*He grasps* **MRS. WOODLAWN** *by the shoulder as if to throw her out of the way, but is intercepted by* **MR. WOODLAWN**.)

MR. WOODLAWN. Kent!

(**KENT** *is startled.* **MR. WOODLAWN** *takes the rifle from his hands.*)

KENT. Don't interfere with this, Woodlawn.

MR. WOODLAWN. Get out! Get off my land!

(*There is a moment's awkward hesitation. Finally* **NATE** *and* **MCCANTRY** *take hold of* **KENT**'s *arms.*)

NATE. Come on, Melvin. No use to stir things up among our own.

KENT. You're a fool, Woodlawn! I'm just tryin' to save lives here. What're you gonna do? Ask this savage to supper?

McCANTRY. All right, Melvin. It's over. Let's go.

(They exit. **MR. WOODLAWN** *glances toward* **CADDIE***.)*

MR. WOODLAWN. Caddie?

CADDIE. I went to the Dakota camp, Father. They weren't planning any massacree.

MR. WOODLAWN. I suspected as much.

(He slowly kneels and places the rifle on the floor. He then rises and steps away. **JOHN***, likewise, cautiously returns his knife to his belt.* **MR. WOODLAWN** *steps forward, extending his hand.* **JOHN** *accepts it, and they shake.)*

Thank you, John, for bringing Caddie back safely. Pilamayaye. Now, you must hurry home. Tiyata kiya.*

JOHN. Good-bye.

*(***CROWD*** parts as* **JOHN** *exits.)*

CADDIE. Father, is it safe to let him go?

MR. WOODLAWN. Don't worry, Caddie. Those men are cowards and fools. By the time Mr. Kent works up enough courage to come back for his rifle, John will be safely back across the river.

MRS. WOODLAWN. Caddie, why ever did you ride to the Dakota camp?

CADDIE. I heard the men talking about attacking John's tribe. Father was gone. I had to warn them.

MR. WOODLAWN. You gave us a bad night, but I think it turned out for the best. We now know there will be peace.

MAGGIE. I told you she was a heroine.

LIDA. Humph! Anyone could have done it, if they had a horse.

---

* For translation, please see Appendix 1 on page 114.

HETTY. *(coming forward)* We never told, Caddie. Not even one word.

KATIE. *(bursting into tears)* We were so frightened!

HETTY. Even when they said you were being scalped, we never told!

CADDIE. Hetty, I'll never call you a tattletale again. And Katie, it took a lot of courage to keep your promise like that. Thank you.

KATIE. I'll never have the courage you have.

CADDIE. I guess there's more than one way to be brave. I just never realized it before.

MR. WOODLAWN. The scare is over, everyone. You can all go home.

MISS PARKER. Harriet, how can we ever repay you for your hospitality?

MRS. WOODLAWN. No need, Hannah. We're neighbors, after all.

MRS. HYMAN. Yes, thank you…and please forgive us for… for the trouble.

MRS. WOODLAWN. *(taking her hand warmly)* Of course.

(SETTLERS gather their things and go. SILAS gives one final whoop.)

SILAS. Bye, Warren.

MAGGIE. Come on, Silas!

LIDA. Wasn't much of a massacree, if you ask me.

JANE. Who asked you?

SILAS. *(making a goofy face)* Yeah!

KATIE. *(lingering at the door with TOM)* Good night, Tom.

TOM. Good night, Katie. Maybe I'll see you tomorrow?

KATIE. That would be nice.

(She exits with her MOTHER as the last of the SETTLERS straggle off. TOM watches her go.)

ANNABELLE. *(entering sleepily)* Where is everyone?

HETTY. Gone home.

ANNABELLE. But what about the massacree?

CLARA. It's over.

ANNABELLE. Over? How perturbing!

WARREN. Where have you been, Annabelle?

ANNABELLE. I have been napping, fortifying myself for the onslaught of hostile aggression. Do you mean to say that the uprising has been subdued already? Someone should have notified me. Were there many casualties?

CLARA. Everyone's safe, thank goodness.

ANNABELLE. Oh, how disappointing to miss my one opportunity at prairie conflict.

MINNIE. I'm sleepy.

CLARA. I'll take them to bed, Mother.

MRS. WOODLAWN. Thank you, Clara.

ANNABELLE. Pray, let me assist.

(**EVERYONE** *exits.*)

MRS. WOODLAWN. Caddie, wait. Perhaps you will help me carry some blankets upstairs.

CADDIE. Yes, Mother.

(There is an uncomfortable silence as **MRS. WOODLAWN** *busies herself collecting bedding.)*

MRS. WOODLAWN. Caroline. People are going to tell you that what you did tonight was a brave and glorious thing. Tom, Warren, the other children.

CADDIE. Father said it was all for the best.

MRS. WOODLAWN. Because it turned out all right in the end. And I suppose what you did *was* brave. But more than that it was foolhardy, reckless, and completely unnecessary.

CADDIE. No! I had to go!

MRS. WOODLAWN. Not with your father and other decent grown men around. But you needed to prove that you knew better than everyone else…you, a child who could hardly understand what was really happening.

CADDIE. I was the only one who *did* understand, I…

MRS. WOODLAWN. Listen to me! You gave me the worst night of my life since Mary's illness. What if the Dakota had been unfriendly? What if one of our men had shot you by mistake? What if John had risked his life to bring you back and before you could explain had been shot and killed?

(**MR. WOODLAWN** *enters quietly and listens unnoticed.*)

CADDIE. But none of those things happened.

MRS. WOODLAWN. That's not the point!

CADDIE. What about you, Mother? You stepped between John and Mr. Kent. You did a brave thing, too.

MRS. WOODLAWN. I felt I had to.

CADDIE. So did I!

MRS. WOODLAWN. And I say you didn't! I've tolerated your wild shenanigans far too long. You're no longer a child, Caddie. Things have got to change.

CADDIE. I'll do as I've always done, as Father has said I might!

MRS. WOODLAWN. Listen to that, Johnny! She's as wild as the countryside. If we were in Boston, such words wouldn't be dreamed of.

CADDIE. Well, we're not in Boston, Mother!

MRS. WOODLAWN. More's the pity! That life is behind us, but there is still a chance in England.

CADDIE. We're all to vote. All of us.

MRS. WOODLAWN. (*pleading*) Take us to England, Johnny. Haven't I tried to be happy here?

MR. WOODLAWN. It means that much to you?

MRS. WOODLAWN. Yes, Johnny, it does.

(**MR. WOODLAWN** *struggles within himself.*)

CADDIE. Father, no!   **MRS. WOODLAWN.** Johnny!

MR. WOODLAWN. (*finally*) Very well, Harriet. I'll write to them tomorrow saying we'll come.

CADDIE. (*betrayed*) I won't go. I hate England because Father was treated badly there. And *I* love it here.

MRS. WOODLAWN. You're tired, Caddie. Tomorrow you'll see it's for the best.

CADDIE. Nothing you think is for the best! I hate you! I hate you!

MR. WOODLAWN. Caddie! Go to your room at once!

CADDIE. How can you let her take us away from Wisconsin? How can you do it?

(She exits in tears. **MRS. WOODLAWN** *moves to her husband in despair.)*

MRS. WOODLAWN. Johnny! Oh, Johnny!

(blackout)

Scene Five

(At Mary's grave, dawn.)

*(**CADDIE** runs on with a bundle of her belongings.)*

CADDIE. I can see the house from here, but they can't see me. Not that they care. Not that they've ever really cared about me at all. They probably wish it was me who died instead of you, Mary. You would have been a real little lady. I'm just a failure as far as they're concerned. Well, they'll be glad now that I'm gone. But I wanted to tell you, Mary, because we're special friends – tell you my plans so you'll know. I'm going to join John and the Dakotas. They'll take me in, I think. We'll travel around a lot, but we'll stop here every once in a while, and I'll come to see you then, I promise. But never down there. I'll never see them again. Maybe when I'm dead, too, they'll hear about it in England somehow and feel pretty bad. But by then - ? Too late. Too late.

*(**ROBERT** appears, coming from the direction of the house.)*

ROBERT. Caddie, lass, what's all this?

CADDIE. I'm leaving, Robert. Leaving forever.

ROBERT. Are ye now? And why, may I ask?

CADDIE. It's Mother. And Father, too. They don't understand me. They want me to "grow up" into something I'm not. So I've got to go away from here.

ROBERT. Now, I am surprised.

CADDIE. Why?

ROBERT. We've known each other for a good long while now, haven't we?

CADDIE. Nearly all our lives.

ROBERT. Yes. And in that time ye've done some amazin' things. Why, ye've befriended the Dakota when ever'one else was pale with fear. Ye've crossed the river when it was over yer head, even though ye couldn't swim. Why, ye single-handedly stopped the massacree by doin' somethin' no man dared to do. I'd gotten this idea about ye, which I guess wasn't so.

CADDIE. What do you mean?

ROBERT. I was of the notion that Caddie Woodlawn didn't let fear stop her from anythin'. Yet, here ye be, on the road outta town, runnin' away from home.

CADDIE. Just because I'm leaving, you needn't think I'm scared of something, Robert.

ROBERT. Aren't ye?

CADDIE. No!

ROBERT. Well, I say ye are. I say it's a small thing to stand up to a bully or ride through the forest to save a friend. That kind o' courage is easily found, when it's necessary. But to face life, and the challenges it offers. Well, that's somethin' that a lot o' people never find the courage to do. And I'm sorely astonished, child, fer I thought ye had the fortitude it takes to grasp at life 'n make it yers. It takes a lion's heart to accept the responsibilities that come with growin' up, Caddie. But ye'll find adventure there, too, new 'n different, excitin' things that a child can never know. But it's only fer the brave, Caddie. And the strong. Not fer frightened children. Or fer those who turn tail 'n run from the changes a-comin'.

CADDIE. You sound like Mother. She doesn't even try to understand the way I feel.

ROBERT. Nor you her neither. Ye've spent most o' yer life learnin' the things that yer father could teach ye. Grant yer mother her rightful turn, and what a splendid woman ye shall become!

*(**CADDIE** makes no reply. **ROBERT** moves as if to leave.)*

Our families...they're our link to forever, lass. A place, no matter how beautiful, is just a place. The sun's up early this mornin'. Lookin' fer the day 'n its brand new promise.

(sings)

MARK HOW THE HILLSIDE IS SILENT AND WAITING
FER SOMETHING ABOUT TO BEGIN.
THE WORLD SEEMS TO PAUSE
AS SOMEWHERE FROM THE VALLEY
A CHANGE IS COMING
A CHANGE IN THE WIND.

AND WHAT SHALL WE DO STANDIN' HERE ON THE HILL,
SO SMALL AND ALONE AS THE STORM RAGES IN?
WE CAN RUN HOME 'N HIDE,
SAFE AND COZY INSIDE,
OR WITH ARMS OPEN WIDE
WE CAN FLY FORTH TO RIDE ON THE WIND!

Think about it, lass. This is a decision ye must make on yer own.

(He pats her shoulder gently and leaves.)

CADDIE. *(sings)*

A CHANGE IS COMING, A CHANGE IN ME.
I WANT TO STAND UP AND SCREAM
THIS IS NOT MY DREAM!
NOT WHAT'S MEANT TO BE!
I WANT TO STAY YOUNG FOREVER,
NOT GROW OLD AND WHITE.
TO DO AS I WISH,
NOT TO WORRY WHAT'S RIGHT.
WANNA RUN THROUGH THE FIELDS,
NOT ROCK BY THE FIRE AND KNIT.
WANT ADVENTURE AND FUN.
GROWING UP DOESN'T FIT IN MY PLAN
AND I DON'T THINK I CAN.

BUT A CHANGE IS COMING, IT CALLS TO ME.
IS THERE SOMETHING NEW
I MUST LEARN TO DO?
I MUST COME TO BE?
A TINY VOICE INSIDE SAYS
IT'S TIME NOW TO FLY,

BUT I WANT TO HOLD BACK,
STILL TOO FRIGHTENED TO TRY!
HAVE I LOST MY OWN WAY
BY RESISTING SO LONG?
AM I MISSING THE POINT
BY IGNORING THIS SONG IN MY HEART?
IS IT TIME NOW TO START?

JUST ONE TINY STEP
YET, SO HARD IN THE TAKING.
I DON'T KNOW QUITE HOW TO BEGIN.
I WANT TO HOLD BACK
IN THE FEAR I MIGHT STUMBLE
IN THE ECHOING RUMBLE
THAT ROARS IN THE WIND!

I STAND AT THE EDGE
OF A WORLD FULL OF CHANGES,
WITH TIME TO DISCOVER
SO MANY NEW THINGS.
AND I KNOW I MUST TRY,
LIFT MY FACE TO THE SKY,
TAKE THE COURAGE TO FLY
TO TRY MY WINGS!

A CHANGE IS COMING, IT'S MEANT TO BE!
BY STANDING STILL
I CAN ONLY KILL
ALL THE LIFE IN ME.
A NEW WORLD WILL OPEN
A CHALLENGE UNKNOWN,
TO CONTINUE ON FOREVER
LONG, LONG AFTER I'VE GROWN.
THE ADVENTURE'S IN CHANGING
NOT IN STAYING THE SAME.
FOR THERE'S MORE TO A PERSON
THAN A CHILD PLAYING GAMES ON A HILL.
ALL RIGHT, MAYBE I WILL.
A CHANGE IS COMING,

A CHANGE IS COMING,
A CHANGE IS COMING,
IT'S IN THE WIND!

(At the end of the song, **MRS. WOODLAWN** *appears.)*

CADDIE. Mother?

MRS. WOODLAWN. Caddie. *(They look at each other a moment, then embrace.)*

CADDIE. I'll try to be happy in England, if that's what you really want. I promise.

MRS. WOODLAWN. No, Caddie. I was wrong last night. We'll vote, just as your father said. The family will decide. Together.

CADDIE. All right.

MRS. WOODLAWN. Please come home now, Caddie.

*(***CADDIE** *nods. They hug, and begin to exit.)*

And Caddie. I love you very much for the loving, courageous child you are. You must always believe that.

CADDIE. Yes, Mother. And just wait 'til you see the splendid woman I shall become.

MRS WOODLAWN. *(Astonished and amused)* Oh yes?

CADDIE. But, might you help me with it? Just a bit?

MRS. WOODLAWN. Why, Caddie Woodlawn. You do amaze me!

(They exit.)

(blackout)

Scene Six

(Interior of the Woodlawn house, later that day.)

*(The **FAMILY** is gathered, each tense with excitement.*
MR. WOODLAWN *enters with* **MRS. WOODLAWN**.*)*

MR. WOODLAWN. As you know, each of you is being asked to take part in the decision we must make. Each person shall write "stay" or "go" on a piece of paper that shall then be placed between the leaves of the family Bible.

MRS. WOODLAWN. Think carefully, children. Ask yourselves, "What will be best for my future? Where shall I be most useful and happy?"

*(***MR. WOODLAWN*** hands out paper.)*

ANNABELLE. I shall write to you all regularly in England. Cordelia Endicott needn't speak of her precious Paris with such superiority again, for I shall have relations of noble descent! How she'll pout, poor thing!

(She laughs with delight, as **ROBERT** *enters.)*

ROBERT. Excuse me, Mr. Woodlawn, but Caddie has a visitor from the Dakota camp.

CADDIE. John?

MR. WOODLAWN. Welcome him in, Robert.

ROBERT. Yes, sir.

(He exits as **JOHN** *enters.)*

CADDIE. Hau koda, John.

JOHN. Hau koda, Little Red Hair.

CADDIE. Did you want to see me?

JOHN. *(nodding solemnly) Ha.* I am going with *oyate*…my tribe.

CADDIE. Where?

JOHN. *(pointing off) Heciya.**

CADDIE. Will you be gone long?

---

* For translation, please see Appendix 1 on page 114.

JOHN. *(nodding his head)* Ha. This is for you. *Upi Yake.**

   (He hands her his belt.)

CADDIE. *Upi Yake?* Your father's belt? For me?

JOHN. *Yuha.* Keep it, Little Red Hair. Until I am here again.

CADDIE. But John, I'm not sure I can. When you come back, we may be gone.

JOHN. Where?

CADDIE. Far away. Not in Wisconsin anymore.

JOHN. *(touching his heart and indicating it is sad)* Cante. Iyokisice. My heart is sad.*

CADDIE. *Cante. Iyokisice.* So is mine.*

   *(***JOHN*** *moves to* **MR. WOODLAWN.***)*

JOHN. You are a good chief. Your people will miss you.

MR. WOODLAWN. Good-bye, John.

   (They shake hands. **JOHN** *moves on to* **MRS. WOOD-LAWN.***)*

JOHN. Little Red Hair learns courage from her mother. *Pilamayaye.* Thank you.

   *(***MRS. WOODLAWN*** *grasps* **JOHN***'s hand.* **JOHN** *moves back to* **CADDIE.** *He hands the belt to her.)*

   Keep this, Little Red Hair. Until we meet again.

CADDIE. *Ha.* Until we meet again.

   *(***JOHN*** *again gestures that his heart is sad.* **CADDIE** *silently returns the gesture.* **JOHN** *leaves.)*

MR. WOODLAWN. *(gently)* Has everyone finished voting?

MINNIE. *(hurriedly scribbling as others place their votes in the Bible)* Just a minute, Father!

MR. WOODLAWN. And now, for the count.

   (reading the papers, one at a time)

   Stay. Stay. Stay. Go. Stay. Stay. Stay. Stay.

WARREN. Hooray!

---

*For translation, please see Appendix 1 on page 114.

MR. WOODLAWN. *(looking with concern to* **MRS. WOODLAWN***)* Only one person voted to go.

CLARA. That one's mine. Give it here and I'll tear it up. I don't want to go to England, either. Not really.

*(***EVERYONE*** cheers.)*

MR. WOODLAWN. Harriet, are you sure? Did you do this for my sake?

MRS. WOODLAWN. No, Johnny, I did it for myself. I never knew how much I loved it here until I had to choose. Better than England – better than Boston. Wherever you and the children are – that's my home.

(She bursts into tears and flings herself into **MR. WOODLAWN***'s arms.)*

TOM. Hooray for Mother!

CADDIE. Hooray for Wisconsin!

(All cheer.)

(blackout)

EPILOGUE

(On the porch, that evening.)

(ROBERT *sings a mournful tune.* **CADDIE** *sits quietly listening.)*

ROBERT.

> EVERY CRICKET ON THE HILL
> BIDS ITS MERRY VOICE BE STILL,
> FOR THE ECHO OF A HAMMER IS A-RINGIN'.
> AND BY MORNIN' TIDE WE'LL SEE
> STRAIGHT AND TALL, THE GALLOWS TREE,
> AND BY NOON ITS BITTER FRUIT
> WILL BE A-SWINGIN'.
>
> WELL TO MAGGIE AND NELL
> OH, I BID YE FARE THEE WELL.
> SHED A TEAR FOR THIS YOUNG LIFE
> TORN ASUNDER!
> AND TO MOLLY AND MAY
> DON'T FORGET ME IN A DAY,
> AS ME BONES LIE, COLD AND GRAY
> SIX FEET UNDER

WARREN. Clara! Clara? Caddie, have you seen Clara? I need help with my embroidery.

CADDIE. Embroidery?

WARREN. Yeah. Tom saw you learning how to do it this afternoon and he said he reckoned he could do it as well as you. And if Tom can do it, I just bet I can, too. Clara! Clara!

(He exits.)

CADDIE. *(taking in the dark sky)* Isn't it beautiful, Robert?

ROBERT. *(also looking up)* A little piece o' forever.

CADDIE. But isn't it the most beautiful night there ever has been? There must be a million stars out. There's the North Star, and the Big Dipper. Can you smell the clover in the meadow, Robert? And the new hay in the field?

ROBERT. That I can.

CADDIE. It all seems stronger and brighter and closer tonight. Is it different? Or is it me? Have I changed, Robert?

ROBERT. In a thousand little ways, lass.

CADDIE. You know, Robert, I think folks keep growing from one person to another all their lives. And life is just a lot of everyday adventures, and, well, whatever life is, I'm ready for it.

ROBERT. Well said, Caddie.

(**CHARLIE ADAMS** *enters with his* **WIFE** *and* **DAUGHTER**.)

ADAMS. Pardon me, sir. Are you the owner of the house?

ROBERT. Sure 'n' I'm the hired hand, sir. I'll fetch Mr. Woodlawn fer ye.

(He exits.)

MILDRED. Is this our new home, Pa?

MRS. ADAMS. Hush, Mildred.

MILDRED. *(moving to* **CADDIE**) Hello. I'm Mildred Adams. We're new here. Who are you?

MRS. ADAMS. Mind your manners, Mildred. Remember, you're a young lady.

MILDRED. I'm not! I'm a Dakota Chief!

(She starts to gallop around the yard, but is stopped by the entrance of **MR.** *and* **MRS. WOODLAWN**.)

ADAMS. *(shaking hands with* **MR. WOODLAWN**) Sir, I'm Charlie Adams. We're sorry to bother you at this time of night, but I'm afraid we've lost our way.

MR. WOODLAWN. I see your wagon, Mr. Adams. Are you planning to settle hereabouts?

ADAMS. Yes, sir. First thing tomorrow, we'll start building the house.

MRS. WOODLAWN. Mrs. Adams, you look dead tired, poor thing. You must all spend the night with us. Johnny will set you on your way in the morning.

MRS. ADAMS. Thank you. I'll admit it's been a long, hard journey.

MRS. WOODLAWN. Where do you hail from, Mrs. Adams?

MRS. ADAMS. Baltimore.

MRS. WOODLAWN. I'm from Boston, myself.

MRS. ADAMS. Oh dear, how have you ever managed in this uncivilized wilderness?

MRS. WOODLAWN. *(laughing)* Don't worry, Mrs. Adams. Wisconsin will grow on you. One day you'll wake up and wonder how you could ever have lived in Baltimore for so long.

(EVERYONE exits into the house, except ROBERT. He breathes in the night air, and sings.)

ROBERT.
AND SUMMERS GLOW
AND COME AND GO,
AND WINTERS BLOW
AND COME AND GO.
AND ALL CHILDREN GROWN
WILL LULLABY THEIR OWN
WITH THE AGE-OLD SONGS
SWEET SUNG ANEW.

*(Slowly, he begins whistling the tune to **A CHANGE IN THE WIND**. He smiles at the audience, shrugs, and strolls off into the darkness.)*

(blackout)

End of Play

APPENDIX #1 – JOHN'S DIALOGUE TRANSLATED

Cante	*(chun-day)*	Heart
Ha	*(hahn)*	Yes
Hau koda	*(hah-oo koh-dah)*	Hello friend
Heciya	*(hay-chee-yah)*	In that direction
Hiya	*(hee-yah)*	No
Inahni	*(ee-naw-gnee)*	Hurry
Iwakta ye	*(ee-wahk-dah yea)*	Beware
Iyaye	*(ee-yah-yea)*	Leave
Iyokisice	*(ee-yoh-kee-shee-chay)*	Sad
Napeyuze	*(nah-pay-yue-zay)*	Shake hands
Okokipe	*(oh-koh-kee-pay)*	Danger
Oyate	*(oh-yah-day)*	Tribe
Pilamayaye	*(pee-lah-mah-yah-yea)*	Thank you
Taku yaka	*(dah-kue yah-kah)*	What do you mean?
Tiyata kiya	*(dee-yah-day kee-yah)*	Toward home
Upi yake	*(ue-pee yah-kay)*	Belt
Wacagnus	*(wah-nchahg-neesh)*	Right now
Wakinyan towa pi	*(wah-kee-yahn doh-nwahn-pee)*	Lightning
Waste	*(wah-shday)*	Good
Yuha	*(yue-hah)*	Keep

PROP LIST

PROLOGUE
Hammers (Settlers)
Saws (Settlers)
Paint Buckets and Brushes (Little Tom, Little Warren, Settlers)
Rustic Sawhorses
Bible (Tanner)
Pennywhistle (Robert)
Two Flintlock Rifles (John, John's Friend)
Springlock Rifle (Mr. Woodlawn)
Gun (Melvin)
Several Pies and Loaves of Bread (Mrs. Woodlawn, Clara)
Handmade Doll (Dakota child)
Small Pine Tree (Settlers)
Timbers (Settlers)

ACT I, SCENE 1
Flower (Mrs. Woodlawn)
Flower (Little Caddie)
Flower (Caddie)

ACT I, SCENE 2
Barrel (On set)
Firewood (Robert)
Hazelnuts (Warren)

ACT I, SCENE 3
Table Setting for 9 (On set)
Silverware (Minnie, Hetty)
Letters (Mrs. Hyman)
2 Extra Table Settings (Minnie, Hetty)
Water Pitcher (Robert)
Hazelnuts (Caddie)

ACT I, SCENE 4
Harmonica (Robert)
Apple (Warren)
Letter (Mrs. Woodlawn)
Barrel (On set)

ACT I, SCENE 5

Nosegays (Minnie, Hetty)
Trunks and Traveling Cases (Mr. Woodlawn, Robert)
Cake of Salt (Warren)
Sheep Puppets (Crew)
Egg (Tom)

ACT I, SCENE 6

Binoculars (Annabelle)
Purse (Annabelle)
Water pail (Robert)
Knife and Rope (Hetty)

ACT I, SCENE 7

Binoculars (Annabelle)
Sketchpad and Pencil (In Annabelle's purse)
Scalp Belt (John)
Raft (On set)
Wooden Pegs (On raft)

ACT II, SCENE 1

Book (Caddie)
Baskets (Minnie, Clara)
Mail (Robert)
Caroline Table (On set)
Rifle (Melvin)

ACT II, SCENE 2

Quilts, Blankets, Carpet Bags, Bundles (Settler Women)
Rifles (Settler Men)
Clothing Bundle (Katie)
Water pail (Tom)
Quilt and Pillow (Clara)
Blankets (Caddie)
Carved Wooden Doll (Tom)
Blankets (Mrs. McCantry)
Ladle (Mrs. Hyman)

ACT II, SCENE 3

Rifles (Melvin, Nate, Ezra)
Bridle (On set)

ACT II, SCENE 4

2 Milk Pails (Robert)

Broom, Mop, Fireplace Poker (Miss Parker, Mrs. Hyman, Mrs. McCantry)

Rifle (Melvin)

Knife (John)

Bedding (On set)

ACT II, SCENE 5

Traveling Bundle (Caddie)

ACT II, SCENE 6

8 Slips of Paper (Mr. Woodlawn)

Scalp Belt (John)

Family Bible (On set)

EPILOGUE

Embroidery (Warren)

COSTUME PLOT

CADDIE – calico dress, petticoat, boots/new dress, petticoat, boots/ dress, petticoat, boots/Add shawl

MRS. WOODLAWN – plain, but attractive dress, petticoat, apron, boots/ Add black shawl/Blouse, skirt, petticoat, apron, boots/attractive dress, petticoat, boots, hat/Blouse, skirt, petticoat, boots

CLARA – pretty calico dress, petticoat, apron, boots/Add black shawl/ feminine dress, apron, petticoat, boots/pretty new dress, petticoat, boots/Add full apron

HETTY – frilly dress, pinafore, petticoat, boots, sunbonnet/ calico dress, petticoat, boots, hair ribbons/dress, petticoat, pinafore, boots, sunbonnet

MINNIE – dress, pinafore, petticoat, boots/ calico dress, petticoat, boots, hair ribbons/ Add pinafore

ANNABELLE – traveling suit with 88 black buttons, 2nd bodice that is missing 88 buttons, stylish hat, mitts, boots/safari outfit, petticoat, boots/ Stylish dress, petticoat, mitts, hat, boots

MRS. HYMAN – overly frilly calico dress, nicely trimmed hat, petticoat, boots/Add black shawl/Fancy dress, petticoat, petticoat, nicely trimmed hat, boots/Dress, petticoat, boots, shawl, bonnet

KATIE HYMAN – lacy dress, petticoat, boots, hair ribbons/ pretty dress, petticoat, boots, bonnet

MISS PARKER – blouse, skirt, petticoat, boots, bonnet/Add black shawl/ dress, petticoat, boots, shawl, hat

LITTLE CADDIE – calico dress, pinafore, petticoat, boots/Add black shawl

LITTLE HETTY – plain dress, pinafore, petticoat, boots, sunbonnet, boots/Add shawl

MARY WOODLAWN – plain dress, pinafore, petticoat, boots

MAGGIE BUNN – calico dress, petticoat, boots, bonnet

LIDA SILBERNAGLE – dress, pinafore, petticoat, boots, bonnet

MRS. MCCANTRY – blouse, skirt, apron, sunbonnet, petticoat, boots/ Add shawl/ dress, apron, petticoat, boots, bonnet

JANE FLUSHER - plain dress, petticoat, boots, bonnet

MILDRED ADAMS – plain dress, petticoat, boots

MRS. ADAMS – plain dress, petticoat, boots, shawl, bonnet

GIRL – calico dress, pinafore, petticoat, boots, sunbonnet/Add shawl

SETTLER #1 - calico dress, petticoat, sunbonnet, boots/Add shawl

LITTLEST CHILD – calico dress, petticoat, boots, hair ribbons/Add shawl

DAKOTA CHILD - dressed in Dakota garb – top, skirt, moccasins

MR. WOODLAWN'S MOTHER (DANCER) – shabby blouse, skirt, shawl, hat

TOM – plain shirt, pants, boots, hat/ dress pants, nice shirt, vest, hat, boots/ shirt, pants, hat, boots

WARREN – plaid shirt, pants, boots, hat/ dress pants, nice shirt, vest, hat, boots/ shirt, pants, hat, boots

ROBERT IRETON – work shirt, work pants, hat, boots, suspenders/Add jacket/ work shirt, work pants, vest, boots, hat

MR. WOODLAWN – work pants, shirt, vest, hat, boots/Add jacket/Dark suit, white shirt, string tie, boots

REVEREND TANNER – black pants, black coat, white shirt, black vest, preacher's collar, boots

JOHN – dressed in Dakota garb – pants, shirt, moccasins, scalp belt

MELVIN KENT – dirty undershirt, dusty work pants, hat, boots, suspenders/Add rugged jacket

NATE CUSTIS – plain shirt, frontier coat, rough pants, boots, hat/ Remove frontier coat

EZRA MCCANTRY - farmer shirt, work pants, vest, farmer's hat, boots/ Add jacket

LITTLE TOM – pants, shirt, shoes, hat, suspenders

LITTLE WARREN – pants, shirt, shoes, hat, vest

OBEDIAH JONES - plaid shirt, overalls, no shoes, hat

ASHUR JONES – undershirt, overalls, no shoes, hat

SILAS BUNN – shirt, pants, suspenders, boots, hat

CHARLIE ADAMS – work pants, work shirt, coat, hat, boots

BOY – plain shirt, brown pants, boots, hat, vest

SETTLER #2 – work pants, plain shirt, frontier jacket, hat, boots

JOHN'S FRIEND – dressed in Dakota garb – pants, shirt, moccasins

MR. WOODLAWN AS A CHILD (DANCER) plain shirt, jacket, breeches, clogs, cap

MR. WOODLAWN'S GRANDFATHER (DANCER) Fancy suit, fancy necktie, hat, boots

SMALL CHILD SOLOIST – plain shirt, pants, boots, suspenders

SET PLOT

PROLOGUE   grassy bank, hillside backdrop exterior of Woodlawn
                house, farmland backdrop, sawhorses, building
                materials

ACT I, SCENE 1 grassy bank, hillside backdrop, grave marker

ACT I, SCENE 2 porch, barrel, farmland backdrop (Can be part of
                exterior of Woodlawn house or In One in front of
                grand curtain.)

ACT I, SCENE 3 interior of Woodlawn house, dinner table

ACT I, SCENE 4 porch, barrel, farmland backdrop (Can be part of
                exterior of Woodlawn house set or In One in front
                of grand curtain)

ACT I, SCENE 5 exterior of Woodlawn house, fence, cornfield, farm
                land background

ACT I, SCENE 6 outside, hillside backdrop

ACT I, SCENE 7 riverbank, woodland backdrop, raft

ACT II, SCENE 1 interior of Woodlawn house with Caroline table

ACT II, SCENE 2 exterior of Woodlawn house, fence, cornfield, farm
                land drop

ACT II, SCENE 3 exterior of Woodlawn house, fence, cornfield, farm
                land drop

ACT II, SCENE 4 interior of Woodlawn house

ACT II, SCENE 5 grassy bank, hillside backdrop, grave marker

ACT II, SCENE 6 interior of Woodlawn house

EPILOGUE   porch, barrel, farmland backdrop (Can be part of
                exterior of Woodlawn house set or In One in front
                of grand curtain)

CPSIA information can be obtained at www.ICGtesting.com
Printed in the USA
LVOW10s0900300516

490466LV00020B/618/P